Night Crawle

MW00906961

Book three in the series: Night Crawlers

By

Ron L. Carter

Copyright 2021 by Ron L. Carter

***

Disclaimer

The people and places appearing in this book, as well as the story, are fictitious. Any resemblance to real people, living or dead, is entirely coincidental.

* * *

Contents

***

Introduction

As soon as Ashley shot Cooper, she let out a scream and dropped the gun. When it hit the carpet, it bounced a few feet away as she wrapped her arms around him. Ashley held onto him until he got too heavy for her to bear. She grimaced in pain as he dropped dead to the floor. She stood there for several seconds, seemingly confused, as the police knocked on the front door a few times. Time seemed to move slowly for that short period as she blocked out everything around her. She didn't even realize the frantic police officers were trying to get into the house. Her mom was also shocked as she screamed out and stood there watching in horror as everything began to unfold.

In his delusional thinking, her father believed Ashley's kidnappers had returned to get her again. As Cooper came running through the door, her father entered the kitchen and grabbed his wife's loaded gun. While Cooper was shouting and waving his gun around, her father took a wild shot at him, but the bullet missed him. It was only inches from his head and landed on the wall behind him.

A few minutes later, the police officers finally busted the door open. Before Ashley or her mother could get the gun from her father, he took a wild shot at the first officer to come through the door. The officer immediately reacted and returned the gunfire with two of his own. Two bullets hit Ashley's father in the chest, and he instantly fell dead to the floor. Her mother continued screaming and crying as she ran to his side and bent down over his body. Realizing what happened to her father, Ashley snapped out of her temporary trance. She started to scream at the sight of her father lying on the floor in a pool of blood.

She yelled to the officer, "You killed my father; you killed the wrong person." She pointed toward Cooper's body on the floor and yelled, "It's him that you're after."

It took a few minutes for the officers to figure out what had happened. After they found out Cooper was dead and they killed the wrong person, they lowered their guns. The police officer that shot her father said, "I'm sorry, miss, but he took a shot at me as soon as I came through the door. I didn't know who he was, but lucky for me, he missed. I was only reacting and protecting myself. I'm sorry I killed your father."

Through the tears and sobbing, she said, "I know, officer, he has some mental issues and thought you were a bad person that had come to harm us. It's not your fault." After they figured everything out, the police called the coroner's office and reported the two deaths. A couple of officers stayed with Ashley and her mom until the coroner arrived.

The following week, Ashley and her mom went through Cooper's simple cremation burial and her father's complete services and funeral. It was an emotional time for both of them. Ashley had lost a father and the man she loved, and her mom lost a husband she'd been with for years. After a few weeks of grieving, they decided to visit her father's grave and take some flowers to leave at his headstone. It was a sunny spring day, with a slight breeze coming from the northwest and not a cloud in the sky. Ashley felt awful for her mom because her mom and dad had been together since they were both sixteen.

Once they got home, they sat at the kitchen table, holding each other's hands and crying. Ashley felt terrible that her boyfriend was responsible for her father's death and that she was the one who had brought him into her mom and dad's lives. She said, "I'm sorry, mom, I had no idea he would do something that crazy and show up at our house after shooting a police officer."

She didn't know why but at that moment, she felt compelled to tell her mom about being five months pregnant with Cooper's child. When Ashley first told her mom, she gasped and quickly jerked her hand away from Ashley's. She looked at her daughter with hatred on her face. Suddenly Ashley was staring into a face she didn't recognize because she'd never seen her mom so angry. Usually, her mom is the stable one, calm and collected, no matter the situation. Then her mom began to scream out things she could never take back.

Her mom's voice sounded as though it was in a deep well as she yelled out, "I hate you; this is all your fault that your father is dead. It would help if you never had come back and brought that monster into this house. He was pure evil from the beginning, and you knew it the entire time. You knew he was no good. You must get rid of that baby because it will be pure evil, just like its father. If you plan to keep it, I don't want anything to do with you anymore. You can find someplace else to live and raise that little monster."

Ashley was stunned by the things her mom was saying to her. Her mom had coddled and petted her and given her unconditional love during the past few years she had been home again.

She put her hands to her mouth until she could say, "I don't believe in killing a baby, so abortion is not an option for me. I will have this baby, regardless of how you feel about it."

Her mom yelled, "Then get your things and get out of my house."

The things her mom said were cutting through her like a knife to the heart. Large tears began to roll down her face. All she could think was that she was sorry as she squeezed out the words a little above a whisper, "I'm sorry, mom. I never wanted this to happen." Suddenly feeling empty and again abandoned by her mom, she quickly got up from the table and ran to her room.

She was now utterly alone, once again, as she shut and locked the door behind her. She couldn't believe her mom had reacted the way she did toward her. She thought they had a loving and caring relationship with each other. She never knew her mom felt the way she did about her and Cooper's relationship. Her mom never indicated how she thought about Cooper as a person or had no future for her daughter. Ashley was suspicious, but her mom confirmed what she feared the most. Since she had returned from being captive, she believed her mom resented her for coming home after all those years away. Since being home, Ashley felt she had intruded on her mom and dad's life. She never told her mom or dad that she had unconsciously blamed them for not coming and finding her. Feeling they just gave up searching for her and accepted her fate. She always wondered why they didn't try harder to see her. She wasn't that far away from where they lived.

Sitting on the bed and crying, she was troubled and confused about what she should do next. She realized she had to leave her mom's home and never come back. But the question was, where would she go? She had never known any place but Ridgecrest since she was born.

She knew she would never feel the same toward her mom after discovering how she truly felt about her. While she packed her things in two suitcases, her mom came to the door and knocked a few times and tried to get her to let her in the room to talk. Her mom's words hurt Ashley, so she refused to let her in the room. She knew nothing she could say would change or make things right between the two of them.

Ashley had received a great deal of money from the crime victim's fund due to her kidnapping ordeal. She put her bank account and cash in her purse and readied to leave. Packing and getting things ready, she was heartbroken, crying, and sometimes even sobbing.

After midnight, she finally pulled it together and told herself she could do this. After her mom had gone to her room, Ashley quietly snuck out the front door with the two suitcases.

A few years earlier, she had bought herself a used 2010 Camry vehicle, so she put the suitcases in the trunk and started the engine. A light came on in her mom's bedroom. She watched from the window corner as Ashley backed out of the driveway.

It was early morning, and the air was brisk and cold. Ashley was wearing a thick coat and gloves as he left. She still had enough money from the Victims Fund to get a fresh start in a new town away from her mom and Ridgecrest. She wasn't sure where she was going but knew staying with her mom another minute was not an option.

***

Chapter 1 – Apartment, Job, and Child Abuse

As Ashely left Ridgecrest, she shivered with moments of fear at the thought of being all alone in the world. Now she didn't have anyone to lean on for support. There were tears in her eyes, and she kept wiping them away with the sleeve of her blouse as she drove out of town. She was also angry, but the anger was mainly from the hurt and pain she felt deep in her heart for her mom not supporting her when she needed her the most. It brought back all the sad memories of her feelings during the seven lonely and painful years she was held captive at the little cabin in the desert. It was where the pedophile sex offender Charlie had held her captive. Now all those feelings had come back to haunt her once again. She had never been away from Ridgecrest for a very long period, even in the old cabin, but considered it her home.

Once she left Ridgecrest, she swore never to return to see her mom again. She kept saying, "I hate you, I hate you, as she drove along, thinking about the things her mom said. She felt her mom's words had cut her too deep to forgive her for those hurtful things.

As she drove along the highway, it was as if she was in a trance. She just blankly stared at the road and kept moving. She turned left on Highway 395 and went south until she reached Highway 58, heading west. She decided to take that route and see where it would lead. She drove through the winding mountainous road without even taking a break. Once she came to Bakersfield, she figured it was as good as any place to settle down, and the town was much larger than Ridgecrest.

She rented a hotel room for a few nights and then started looking for a place to live. After searching the for-rent ads, she grabbed a paper and found a little furnished apartment on the south/east side of town. It wasn't in the best of neighborhoods, but it was one she felt she could afford. It was in a large apartment complex with over 200 other units. Half were ground-floor apartments, and the other half were second-story units; she could get one on the ground floor. The apartment complex had a dark green wooden exterior, and the trim around the windows and doors was painted white. They had been there for a while because the outside trees and plants were full-grown and well-maintained. They blended in well with the buildings. Some of the large bushes were almost right against the building's wooden exterior, making the place feel safe.

After putting money down on the apartment and settling in, she took a few days to acclimate to the town. She began to explore and find out where she could locate the shopping centers and other parts of the city.

After a few days of feeling comfortable, she went to the local restaurants to look for work because she didn't want to sit idle and do nothing all day. She also had to support herself or eventually run out of money.

After putting in her application to several places, she soon found a server at a local restaurant and began waiting on tables. She had never worked before, but this job was easy for her. She made enough wages and tips to support herself even after her baby was born.

On the eight-month and twenty-seventh day of being pregnant, she gave birth to a seven-pound eight-ounce boy. She and Cooper had talked about the baby's name when she found out she was pregnant. Both agreed that they would name him Jackson if they had a boy. She also decided to give him Cooper's last name Bailey.

She took off work for a few months after he was born and spent a lot of time with him. Even though she loved being a mother and caring for him, she soon had to return to work to support herself and her new son.

She got a young girl named Summer to babysit Jackson while she worked the day shift at the restaurant. Summer was out of school but going back for the fall semester at the local Junior College.

Jackson was an easy baby for her to babysit and did not demand anything out of the ordinary. She cared for him at Ashley's apartment, so he felt safe and secure with her and his surroundings. He was well-adjusted and always happy to see his mom when she got home from work early evening.

Ashley was happy that he appeared to be an average child and did not show any negative signs like Cooper's family. She was always excited and glad to spend time with him. She devoted her every spare moment to him when she was home. She carried him around on her hip with one arm wrapped around him and did her housework with the other arm. She never left him alone when she was home. She teased and played with him as you do with babies. She showed him constant care and love, like most mothers do with their children.

When he was about seven months old, the college's fall semester was ready to begin, so Summer had to go back to school. She could no longer take care of him. Ashley started searching for a replacement when one of her neighbors named Margret, whom she had befriended, volunteered to take care of him for a small daily fee. In her late twenties, she was five feet nine inches tall and a little overweight but friendly, outgoing, and likable. Margret was raising four young children alone after her husband had left her. She had two boys, ages 5 and 6, and two daughters, ages 2 and 3. Ashley didn't check on her neighbor's qualifications to watch after Jackson because the price was affordable for her. She also mistakenly figured that since she had four children and appeared to be a good mother, she would be the perfect person to take care of her son.

She didn't know it then, but he began to get abused from the first day she dropped him off at Margret's apartment. She didn't harm him herself, but her two young sons were the culprits. In the beginning, they would harass him and make fun of him.

Their mother had forced the boys to stay in the room with him and watch after him while she went about her housework chores and taking care of her two younger daughters. The boys voiced their displeasure about being his babysitter, but Margret wouldn't listen to them. They had no choice in the matter, and she forced them to stay in the room with him the entire day.

Every day after she dropped him off, Margret would immediately take him to a highchair in the middle of the boy's room. She then gave him a sippy cup full of milk and a handful of cereal she would put on the tray in front of him. She would then shut the door behind her, leaving the boys alone with him. They resented that their mom had taken on Jackson's care during the day, leaving them to care for him. They felt like it was punishment for them. They wanted to play outside or do other things normal kids do.

They tried their best to get out of watching him, but their mom ignored their pleas. When they tried, she said, "If you don't take care of him, then I'll come in here with a belt and beat your little asses. Do you understand me?"

The boys didn't want that, so they reluctantly said, "Yes, mom, we understand."

Because of their daily and constant anger at their mom over the issue, they began to take out their frustration on Jackson. At first, their abuse began with simple scary faces they would make toward him to get him to cry. Then, as it progressed, it went to pulling his hair, yelling at him, and calling him names.

Over the next few months, they sometimes bit and pinched him without leaving a mark as they worsened. While the boys harassed and tormented him, his little mouth would be wide open as he screamed aloud. No matter how loud he cried, Margret ignored his screams for help. Things got so out of hand with the boys that he would start crying as soon as his mom dropped him off at the apartment. Jackson sometimes sobbed all day long while in the room with them until his mom picked him up after work. On most days, he could only whimper deep heartfelt sobs while gasping for breath. It was horrible abuse and pure hell for him.

Sometimes, the boys took Jackson out of the highchair and put him on their bed. They would jump up and down until bouncing him high in the air. They would laugh about what they were doing the entire time they did that. Several times, they jumped him off the bed and onto his head on the floor. Each time it happened, he would be temporarily stunned by the impact of the fall before he regained his senses and started screaming out in pain. As soon as he started screaming, the boys quickly grabbed him and put him back in the highchair. They tried to do it before their mom came rushing in like a crazy person to see what they had done.

Watching him react the way he did made the boy's evil actions intensify. They developed a deep hatred for him and tried to make his life as miserable as possible. They were hoping their mom would stop taking care of him. The more he cried, the worse the boy's torment and abuse became. Margret either didn't care about what they were doing or didn't want to know. She ignored his crying and screaming all day long unless it became too intense for her and she couldn't take it anymore. It was as though once the door was closed, the kids were no longer her concern for her unless things got out of control. She did go into the room at least twice a day. Once to give Jackson something to eat for lunch and another time to change his diaper. She usually changed it just before his mom came to get him.

Occasionally when she heard the boys yelling loudly, she would open the door and ask them what they were doing to him. They constantly lied to her and told her they were playing a game with each other. If she had been doing her job, she would've seen Jackson crying out in fear because he was terrified of the boys. She was either too occupied with herself or didn't care.

After about three months of continuous abuse, Ashley began to wonder why his eyes were puffy and swollen when she picked him up at the end of the day. She also couldn't understand why he would cling to her for dear life as soon as he saw her. Not having any experience raising a child, Ashley thought that maybe he couldn't deal with her going to work every day and leaving him with a babysitter. She also believed that perhaps he had become overly attached to her and felt abandoned when she left him there. She never dreamed he was abused by the boys and neglected by Margret for a million years.

After she first noticed his emotional state, she became aware that something was wrong. After a few weeks, she wondered why Jackson was getting worse. He started to scream and start crying uncontrollably every time before they even got to Margret's apartment each day. When it became a chore for her to drop him off at the apartment, she confronted Margret that something was wrong. She asked Margret if everything was ok with her taking care of him. Margret asked her why she was concerned about things. Ashley said he was acting a little differently than before. She told her that Jackson was overly emotional when dropping him off and again when she picked him up from her apartment.

She said it appeared that he was losing weight instead of gaining it like he should have been. She didn't know that he would have very little to eat on most days because the boys would take his treats and eat them. When their mom wasn't looking, they would throw the rest of his other food in the trash. She told Ashley that she believed everything was ok with him but didn't tell her that he constantly cried when she was at work. She also never said that her two young boys cared for him. If Ashley had known that was the case, she would never have agreed to let Margret babysit him.

The horrible abuse lasted until one night. After picking him up after work, she noticed bruises on his legs and arms. He also had a few teeth marks on his upper left shoulder. When she first saw them, she got angry. She immediately suspected some abuse, grabbed him in her arms, and headed to Margret's apartment. She confronted Margret and asked her how he had gotten so many bruises and teeth marks all over his body. Margret had spent so little time watching him that she didn't even know that one of the boys had bitten him a couple of times on the shoulder. She didn't know about the teeth marks. She also didn't know about the minor pinch mark bruises on his body.

Realizing what her boys had done, Margret instantly made up a lie. She said they were trying to teach him how to walk, and he fell against some furniture. He also claimed that he had bitten one of the boys, and the boy bit him back. She said they were trying to get him not to do that and teach him a lesson not to bite. Ashley was shocked that she would admit to something like that and said, "What, you've got to be kidding me. You can't do that to a baby." She was furious as she stared into Margret's face angrily. She said, "I can't believe you let these things happen to my son. I trusted you."

She stormed out of the apartment and took him home. She bathed him in the sink and looked him over carefully. She then realized that he had tiny yellow bruises from previous abuse marks several days old. That's when she knew he had been going through pure hell while at Margret's apartment. She cried as she dried him off, held him in her arms, and said, "Oh, my God, I'm so sorry, Jackson. I didn't know what they'd been doing to you. I promise it will never happen again. You won't spend another day at the apartment with those little monsters."

After dressing him, she was so upset that she carried him in her arms, went back to the apartment, and screamed out to Margret that she would report her to Child Protective Services for child neglect and abuse. Margret said, "Go ahead. It won't do you any good because they won't do anything about your allegations." Ashley was so angry with her that she said, "You will be lucky if you don't go to jail for what you and your boys have done to my son." He was screaming because he thought she would leave him there with her and the boys again by that time.

She went back to her apartment, and it took several minutes to calm him and herself down. She was so angry that she let him sleep in her bed. She stayed awake all night thinking about what Margret and her boys had done. She was wondering what other hell they had put him through.

***

Chapter 2 – Ashley's Revenge

For the next few days, she felt terrible that she hadn't noticed what Jackson had been going through during the months he was at Margret's apartment. She couldn't believe she hadn't seen the bruises on his body.

She called Child Protective Services, and they sent a person out to talk to her and take a look at him. After Ashley checked him over, the marks on his body were almost gone when the representative came out and examined him. Ashley hadn't taken any pictures of the bruises or teeth indentations on his body, so she didn't have any proof of the abuse.

After talking to Margret and hearing her story, the representative returned and spoke to Ashley. She said, "There is no visual proof of any abuse that may or may not have taken place, so we can't do anything about your allegations. It's her word against yours."

She said to the representative, "Oh, my God, I can't believe this. That woman will get away with all the abuse she and her boys caused my son."

The representative said, "I'm sorry, Ashley, there is nothing I can do. My hands are tied."

She quit her job after learning about Margert and her boys abusing and neglecting her son. After the social worker left, she found another furnished apartment in the north/east part of town and near the downtown business area. She gathered their things and moved from the apartment complex as quickly as possible.

She decided not to work for a few months and just spent time with Jackson to help him with his fears. She wanted him to realize she was there to protect him. He was clinging to her as if he feared for her to get out of sight. He was scared he would face the boy's torture again. He would scream and cry for her if she left him alone in a room because of his fear. She was aware of his father's psychopathic problems and feared he would now be affected for life because of the boy's abuse. She believed the abuse would trigger some of the same psychopathic issues as his dad had.

Once she settled into her new apartment, she couldn't get her mind off what Margret had allowed her boys to do to her son. She couldn't believe her so-called friend had neglected his care. The more time Ashley spent with him, the more her heart hurt for her him. She began to relate her experiences while being held captive and abused to what he had gone through. The thoughts of his abuse started to eat her up inside. She became obsessed with what she believed he must have gone through. She envisioned all kinds of horrible abusive behavior they inflicted on him. Some of her abusive imaginations were true, and some weren't.

When she went to bed at night, she began to relate everything to her experiences. She started having flashbacks of when Charlie kidnapped her at age nine. She cringed at the thought of being held captive in the cabin for all those years. During the flashbacks, Ashley relived a lot of things Charlie had done to her. She became so emotional that she lay in bed and cried as she now thought about them.

It wasn't until Cooper stumbled upon the old run-down place in the desert that and saved her. It changed her life. He and his dog were lost and wandering the desert for a few days. They had gone without water, and things were getting desperate for them. He was trying to get a drink of water for himself, and his dog and Charlie refused to give it to them. Rather than die in the desert, Cooper decided to kill Charlie and take the needed water. Once inside the cabin and killed Charlie, he discovered her in the bedroom bolted to the wall. She had a chain around her wrist that Charlie had attached to the wall.

While lying in bed, she looked down at the indented circle still about a quarter-inch deep around her wrist from the years of wearing the chain. It was her terrible reminder of the horrible torture Charlie had put her through. Looking down and rubbing her wrist, she smiled when thinking about Cooper and the day he released her. She remembered that day as being the happiest day of her life. Then the expression on her face changed from a smile to complete and utter despair. She had anger in her voice as she whispered, "Nobody will hurt my son or me like that ever again. I will kill them if they try."

She blamed Margret for the boy's demonic behavior toward Jackson because she was responsible for his care while Ashley worked. She knew that if Cooper were still alive, he wouldn't let Margret get away with what she allowed his son to endure. She knew that once he learned about her neglect and the boy's abuse, Cooper would've probably killed or hurt her badly. Ashley had been with him when he planned and carried out some of his attacks on the vigilante group. She felt the same as Cooper and had no remorse for what he did to the vigilante guys. She never blamed Cooper for his actions and thought he was justified in getting his revenge upon them. Now she was feeling that same way once again toward Margret.

After wrestling with herself for several days, she decided she wouldn't let her son's torture and abuse go without Margret getting punished for what she allowed to happen to him. Especially after Child Protective Services told her there was nothing they could do about the abuse. She knew it would be up to her to devise some punishment for Margret. She began plotting how and when she could carry out her revenge act, especially without getting caught and going to jail. Ashley had been with Cooper when he took revenge on the vigilante group. She believed she knew how to keep from getting caught.

The following weekend she visited a few yard sales on different streets in town until she could buy an old used wooden baseball bat for a few dollars. It was just what she had been looking for and would work perfectly for what she had planned. She went to a store and purchased charcoal to cover her face, black clothing, and a black hoodie sweatshirt. She also bought a temporary black color for her hair.

She knew that Margret always got a babysitter once a month on a Wednesday night when she played Bunko with some of her girlfriends. She met one of the women from the group once they came to Margret's house and asked her to join them. The woman had given Ashley her phone number. She called the woman, showed interest in the game, and wanted to know when they had their next meeting. She also asked her where the meeting was going to take place. The woman was excited to hear from her, so she quickly gave Ashley the information. Once she discovered the next time Margret was going out to meet up with the Bunko girls, she would be poised and ready to carry out her attack.

On the night of her planned attack, Ashley got a babysitter for a few hours ago for Jackson. She had dyed her hair black before the babysitter arrived and was ready to go. After leaving the babysitter with him, she put on her black clothing and grabbed the black charcoal, gloves, and baseball bat. She laid the bat on the passenger side of the front seat and next to her.

She drove to Margret's apartment building and parked her car several blocks away in a dark, secluded area near a store's dark parking lot. She then waited until it was dark before taking her time and made sure nobody watched her as she put the black charcoal on her face, neck, and hands. She was already wearing the black sweatshirt but put on some gloves and grabbed the bat.

She was shaking like crazy as she crept up within a distance of Margret's front door apartment. The entire time she was making her way to the intended hiding place, she carefully looked around and made sure nobody had seen her making her way into position.

She was only a few feet away from the apartment's front door when she disappeared behind some tall and bushy plants into her hiding place. There was a space between the bushes and the building where she could hide without being seen. It was just large enough for her to stay hidden where nobody could see her. It had an open area where she could jump out quickly when she needed to get out quickly.

Once there, she saw the babysitter come by in front of her and knock on the door. In a short time, Margret met her and invited her inside. After a few minutes after the babysitter's arrival, Margret left her apartment to meet with her friends.

While she was sitting there, she did what Cooper used to tell her and tried hard to control herself and her emotions while waiting and watching the front door. Cooper used to say to her that you can never get impatient when you're waiting for someone. He told her she had to take deep breaths and let them out slowly to calm her nerves. He also told her she couldn't back out once she decided what you would do. You have to go through with your plan, or it could backfire on you, and you could get caught. She had been following his advice, and it seemed to work for her.

She had decided to wait for Margret to return before she carried out her attack. It would be pitch-black outside that night, and the neighborhood would be quiet and calm. None of the neighbors would be just milling outside their apartments that night.

While contemplating her attack, she told herself to control her anger and not kill Margret with the bat when she hit her. Even though she felt like she was angry enough, it could happen. She didn't want to kill her. She just wanted to hurt her and make her suffer physically and emotionally as her son had suffered. She kept telling herself not to say anything during the attack, or Margret would recognize her voice and report her to the police.

As she patiently waited for her to return, she kept taking deep breaths and letting them out slowly to try and calm herself down. She was shaking and nervous the entire time. It was the first time she had done something like this by herself, and she was shaky and scared. She believed the fear somehow heightened her alertness. She could hear police sirens going off deep in the city and every sound of doors closing and opening in the apartment complex. The sounds of the night were exaggerated. She peered out into the vast darkness and realized she was all alone in the world at that moment. Nobody was there to help her or protect him, and she thought, "What a lonely feeling."

After a few hours had passed, it was now ten-thirty when she saw Margret walking briskly back toward her apartment. She figured she was probably a little scared walking alone in the dark or staying out a little longer than she intended.

Ashley's adrenaline was pumping as her heart was beating fast when Margret almost reached her front door. She had just walked in front of her when Ashley instantly sprung out from behind the bushes. It was like a cat upon its prey. Just before she got to her front door, Ashley quickly hit her on the side of the head with the bat. She went down as if to be shot by a gun. It happened so fast that Margret didn't know what had happened to her. She didn't even have time to understand who or what hit her. Once Margret was on the ground, she opened her mouth to scream, and Ashley hit her again hard and knocked her unconscious. This time she was out cold and defenseless. Ashley quickly walloped her across her left upper arm with the bat. She heard the bones crack and snap from the hard blow. Then she promptly did the same thing to her other arm.

After breaking both of Margret's arms, she immediately took off, running toward where she had her car parked. She didn't stop running until she got about four blocks from the apartment complex. Then she heard Margret screaming and knew she wasn't dead, and she had accomplished her goal during her attack. She put the bat down next to her body and quickly made her way to her car.

She jumped in her car and immediately wiped the bat clean of all fingerprints. She then started driving away. Several blocks away, she went through a store parking lot and threw the bat in a dumpster. She drove a few more blocks, parked under a streetlight, and removed all the black charcoal from her face and hands. Once home, she paid the babysitter just as she gathered up her things and left. After the babysitter went home, she checked on her sleeping son and went into the bathroom. She ran a bath and washed out the temporary black color from her hair. She sat in the tub for a few minutes and turned the water on hot and relaxed.

Still reeling with adrenaline and excitement about what she'd done, she went into Jackson's bedroom and took him in her arms as he slept. She whispered, "That bitch should've taken better care of you. At least her life will be miserable for a few months, and that's all I wanted." She chuckled and said, "She won't even be able to use toilet paper to wipe herself until her arms heal. That will cause her enough grief in her life for me. It was worth what I did to her."

About a week later, the police contacted her and wanted to talk to her about Margret's attack. The officer who came to speak with her said the woman she had called on the phone and asked when the next Bunko meeting would take place had told them about the two of them talking. She said Ashley seemed very interested in the next meeting and the time. She admitted to the officer that she did speak to the woman. Telling him about being interested in joining their group but couldn't make it that night. The officer asked her if she had anything to do with the attack. She lied and said, "Of course not. I didn't even know anything happened to Margret until you showed up today and told me something had happened to her.

She asked the officer, "What happened to Margret?" The police officer said someone attacked her and broke her arms with a blunt object, but she survived the attack. She crossed the fingers on one of her hands and told the officer she was happy that Margret was ok.

Ashley was passive-aggressive because of what the Child Protection Representative had said to her when she asked if she had any photos of Jackson's bruises. She calmly asked the officer, "Do you have any proof, like, witnesses, photos, or a video of what happened, officer? The officer said, "No, it happened at night and in the dark, so we don't have anything like that. He thanked her for her time and left. That was the last she ever heard about the attack or Margret.

***

Chapter 3 – Jackson's Younger Years

Ashley decided she would try and find a job as a bartender when she felt Jackson was secure enough so she could go back to work again. She decided she would be with him during the day and then work nights. That way, she could get a babysitter to watch him while he was home, sleeping in his bed while she worked.

He was past the point of crawling and had just started to get his balance and walk. Ashley wanted to take time and teach him how to walk, so it didn't take long, and he walked all over the apartment.

She got a babysitter for a few hours and went to some bars and restaurants until a bartender from one of the bars was good enough to give her a book. It was about how to make any alcohol-mixed drink a person may want. He told her she needed to know how to make mixed drinks before getting a bartending job. It took a few months, but she memorized the book and learned how to make mixed drinks.

After a few weeks of searching and waiting, she worked at a local restaurant with a full bar. They told her she needed to work serving tables first before they would let her be a bartender. The manager told her they would slowly work her in as a bartender if they liked how she worked as a server. It took her a few weeks to get past her probationary period, so they slowly moved her to a part-time bartending position.

When it came to babysitters, she had learned her lesson from using a friend or neighbor to watch her son. She contacted a licensed babysitting agency to watch Jackson instead. It worked out well for her because the agency she used gave her a lot of flexibility. Sometimes she had to work a little later than planned or go in to work a little early.

Although she had the babysitters, it still became a challenge because she worked the night's required late hours at the bar. She would come home and try to get a few hours of sleep before Jackson would wake her early in the morning. He would come and crawl into bed with her and want her to get up and play with him. Even though it was hard the first few years, she struggled and spent a lot of time with him.

The first few years after the experience with Margret were uneventful, as Ashley went to work every day and then came home to be with her son. Jackson was like all normal kids his age and loved spending time with his mom. She also loved that time with him, and the two of them formed a strong mother-son bond during that particular time.

When he was around four years old, she decided to put him in daycare for a few hours a day to be around other kids. It also allowed her to do some shopping and other things while he was there. She could run her errands and grocery shopping during that time.

He was a happy child and always had a smile on his face while he was home. He seemed stable when he was around his mom or his babysitter. However, he had a hard time playing with other kids away from home because of fear. He was afraid they always wanted to hurt him. Ashely felt it was the consequence of what the boys had done to him when he was a baby.

Because of his fear, he became protective of himself. If another child at the daycare he was playing with became aggressive toward him, he would lash out at them. He would bite them or punch them with his fist. He was no longer like he was when he was a baby and just sat there and took the abuse.

The daycare teacher would tell Ashley about what he had done to the other kids when she picked him up at the end of the day. When they got home and were alone, she would ask him what had happened. All he would say to her about them was that the other kids were mean to him. She repeatedly tried to explain to him that he couldn't hurt the other kids. She told him he couldn't bite or hit them whenever he got mad at them. He would always tell her they hit him or bit him first, and he was protecting himself. She had a hard time not believing him but tried. After several complaints from the daycare facility, she finally had to remove him from care because he could never control his anger with the kids.

Then it came time for Jackson to go to Kindergarten when he reached age five. He fought the entire process with his mom because he didn't want to go and be away from her and be around the other kids from school. He felt it was some form of punishment, and he had separation anxiety. To him, it was almost like being abandoned by his mom.

On the third day of school, she drove him there, kissed him, and watched him walk up to the school entry. She then watched him go inside the building before she left. He never made it to his class that day. Once she drove off, he turned around, left school, and took off walking on foot. About an hour later, the school called her and asked her if he was sick because he had never made it to class. She panicked when they told her he wasn't in class because she had dropped him off there.

She said, "What are you saying? I dropped him off at school myself. He has to be there somewhere. Maybe he went to one of the other classrooms."

The principal told her he would check the other classrooms and then call her back. About thirty minutes later, he called and said he wasn't in any of the other classes.

A panic came over her, and she immediately went to her car. He drove as fast as possible to the school. Once there, she frantically searched every schoolroom for him, but he was nowhere. The school reported him missing to the police, and they came out and talked to her about what had happened. After telling them everything, they told her they would begin a search for him. After waiting around for a few hours to see if he had turned up, she was devastated. She left the school dejected and slowly drove home, crying the entire way home. She believed some sick person had kidnapped her son, just like Charlie had done to her. It brought back all those hurtful feelings to her about her kidnapping.

When she got home, she looked toward the front door, and Jackson was sitting on the steps. She couldn't figure out how he'd gotten there but was relieved and happy. She was so relieved that she quickly parked the car, ran, grabbed him, and hugged him. When she asked him how he got home, he said he had walked several blocks from school to the apartment. He had been crying because she wasn't home when he arrived and couldn't reach the locked door. She hugged him for several seconds and breathed a sigh of relief. Then she looked at him angrily and told him she was happy that he was okay, but she never wanted it to happen again. She said he scared her because she thought someone had kidnapped him.

She immediately called the school and the police department and told them he was home. She was angry with the school for not eyeing her son better. She chastised the school principal for what had happened and for letting her son leave the building unattended.

Once she was off the phone with them, she sat him down and told him that he scared her to death and that he would be in big trouble if he ever did something like that again. He had tears in his eyes as he promised her he wouldn't. He told her that he didn't want to go to school. He hated it, and the kids were too mean to him. She was angry when she told him that he would have to get used to it because he was going to school.

That night, before she left for work, she wondered how he knew where they lived and how he could find his way home. They lived almost a mile from the school, and it took a few turns to get to their apartment. That's when she realized he was a very intuitive, intelligent, and gifted child. Most five-year-old kids wouldn't know how to find their way home.

The first few months of school were hell for him and his mom. He got in trouble for attacking the other kids in his class when he said they were mean to him. After several heart-to-heart talks between him and her, she finally convinced him to stay away from the kids he thought were mean. She told him he wouldn't get in trouble for hitting them if he stayed away from them. That's when he developed a loner's behavior, and from that point on, he kept to himself and ignored all the other kids said and did to him. He even stayed out of any school-sponsored sports programs because he couldn't play well with other kids without getting angry with them.

Ashley had to move him from one school to another from first grade through junior high school. No matter how hard he tried, he would always end up in fights with the other boys. He was tough and held his own in a fistfight, even against boys a lot bigger than him. It seemed as though the school's bullies inevitably wanted to try their luck at beating him up, but they, too, had very little chance of succeeding. Sometimes the bullies got the other kids to join in, as several of them would gang up on him. He got along well with the girls in his class and made friends with a few of them along the way. One friend that he liked was Kari Simmons because she was good to him. At home, he continued his loner ways to keep himself occupied by playing video games. He was always on the computer looking things up about things he was interested in learning.

That lifestyle continued for several years of his early life. During that period, Asley took Jackson to a few different psychologists and psychiatrists to see if they could help him with his anger issues. They always told her that he would probably grow out of his problems as he got older. They told her it would help if she worked with him and tried to talk to him about his anger. Ashley had a different belief than the experts. She knew his dad's family history and feared he had inherited some of the sociopathic tendencies they possessed. No matter how much she talked to him about his anger issues, it didn't help. As he got older, he found a way to internalize the anger and keep it to himself.

He was around twelve when she began to leave him by himself at night while she worked instead of paying for a babysitter. That's when he started sneaking around and smoking cigarettes after his mom left for work. He also started smoking Marijuana around that same time. He found that it helped calm his nerves and suppressed some of the anger he possessed. She had gotten him a cell phone, so she could call him any time she wanted to ensure everything was okay with him. He always made sure he had the phone with him if his mom called, and he only stayed out for an hour or so during the night.

That's when he started leaving the house and walking around the neighborhood at night. At first, he wasn't sure what he was looking for, but he liked the freedom to be on his own and do anything he wanted. Sometimes he would walk about a half-mile to the nearest quick-stop store and hang out for a little while. He hid in the dark, where no one could see him, as he watched people come and go from the store. He was fascinated with people and how they acted when they shopped at the store.

As he gained more confidence in being alone at night, he asked customers for a cigarette or a beer. Occasionally, one of the customers would give him one or both before they left. He knew where his mom stashed her weed, and he sometimes took some of it for his use. He liked how the Pot and beer made him feel because they both made him high. He began getting braver with the store's patrons, occasionally saw someone he recognized, and started a conversation with them. If he felt he could trust them, sometimes he would trade them some of his pot for a beer or two.

***

Chapter 4 - Killing the Drug Addict

On one occasion, when Jackson was at the store, an older teenager saw what he was doing by trading pot for beer. He confronted Jackson and slapped him a little before taking his Pot from him. After that day, swearing it would never happen again. He began to carry a thick fourteen-inch-long steel bar with him four inches in diameter for his protection. He drilled a hole near the bottom of it and then ran a heavy shoelace through the hole. He tied the ends of the shoelace together, so it was long enough to get his hand through. He could then wrap it around his wrist and firmly grip the weapon. Once he had it in his hand and secure, nobody could rip the bar out of his hands and beat him with the bar.

As he became braver, he began to creep around to the different neighborhoods at night to see what was happening. Sometimes, when lights were on in a house, he would sneak up to the window and peek inside. He wasn't weird. He just wanted to see what the people were doing with their lives. At the time, he didn't have any malicious intent; it was merely curiosity. He soon realized that most people's lives were dull and unexciting, just like his. He didn't know that a vigilante group shot and killed one of his dad's uncles for peeping into houses at night and watching the girls undress. Sometimes he broke into their homes while the girls were sleeping and got right up next to their beds. He would stand there and watch them sleep.

After several months of exploring a lot of the different neighborhoods, he began to venture out further. Sometimes it took him to some rough areas of town. At almost thirteen, he found himself walking along an unfamiliar street. He was skipping along and enjoying his freedom. Occasionally, he would pick up a rock and throw it at one of the empty buildings, trying to break more class out of one partially broken window.

When he went around one of the corners of a building along the empty street, he accidentally stumbled onto a couple of scruffy-looking guys doing a drug deal with each other. It was a little dark because only one streetlight was working, and it was about a half-block away from where they were standing. The men had just exchanged drugs and money with each other when he walked up on them.

At first, he didn't realize what was happening as he froze in his tracks and just stood there looking at them. The guy that had just gotten his drugs turned and looked over at him and yelled out, "What the fuck are you looking at, kid?" When he said that he began to walk toward Jackson and said, "What are you doing out here in our hood alone at night?" He didn't answer either of the guy's questions because he didn't know what to say, and the questions startled him. He didn't know if he should try to talk to these guys or run.

It seemed to make him angry when he didn't answer the guy. The guy charged at him like he was going to grab him. Jackson began to run away, but to his surprise, the guy started chasing him. He ran after Jackson and yelled, "Hey, you little punk, come back here. I was talking to you. I'm going to kick your ass." He knew he couldn't outrun the guy because he was a lot taller and older. He feared for his life as he whispered, "I can't let this guy catch me. He may beat me up or kill me."

Just as Jackson ran around the corner of an empty building, he had an opportunity. He ducked into a dark empty alley that didn't have any lights. You could hardly see your hands in front of your face. It was so dark. He immediately crouched down behind trash bags and instantly took a defensive position. He pulled out his metal pipe weapon and had it ready. The guy came around the corner, and by then, he was furious. The guy started looking for him and knocking over trash and other things in the alley. He said, "Where are you, kid? I will beat your ass when I get a hold of you." Jackson thought it was weird that the guy wanted to hurt him for walking up to their drug deal.

The guy strained his eyes in the dark to try and see Jackson. He was already stoned and not thinking or acting normally. Jackson was scared as he controlled his breathing when the guy got near him. Once he was close to him, Jackson quickly jumped up from where he was hiding and struck the guy across the side of the head with his pipe weapon. The guy instantly dropped to the ground, and Jackson hit him a couple more times in the head with his bar weapon. He wanted to make sure the guy didn't get up and take the gun away from him and beat him with the thing.

As he looked around to make sure nobody else saw what happened, he quickly went through the guy's pockets and took the drugs and money he had on him. He could tell he had hit the guy too hard during that brief encounter because he wasn't moving. He leaned down and felt for a pulse, but there wasn't any. The guy was dead.

The ordeal shook him up, but he wasn't upset about killing the guy. He sincerely believed that if the guy had grabbed him, he would've beaten him, raped him, or even killed him. Whatever his intentions were, he wouldn't let the guy get his hands on him. He also knew he didn't want to get slapped around as the older teenager had done to him at the quick-stop store. He felt like the guy's death was self-defense.

He quickly looked around the corner of the building to see if the other guy had chased after him. There was nobody in the street, and it was quiet and empty. It was so dark, and he felt a little creeped out, and someone was following him. He left the area as soon as possible, not wanting another encounter like that one. He kept looking over his shoulder to make sure he was alone. He finally made his way back to the area where he was familiar.

As he walked back toward his apartment, he smoked a little pot to calm his nerves and said, "The guy should've left me alone. I didn't do anything to him or his friend. It was crazy that he chased after me and said he wanted to kick my ass. I'm glad I had my weapon with me to protect myself."

***

Chapter 5 - Ashley's New Relationship

Ashley was young, pretty, and had a nice shapely figure and a good personality to go with her looks. The guys drinking at the bar were always teasing her and asking her to go out. She kept her hair long and in a ponytail while behind the bar. When she let it down, the guys would tease her about being a movie star. Although she flirted with the regulars in the bar, she rarely went out with any of them. Her work was steady, and it took care of her financial needs and responsibilities.

Occasionally she would meet a new guy that would come into the bar she had never seen before. If she were attracted to him and liked his personality and asked her out on a date, she would go out with him on her days off. They would go to dinner or catch a movie. Usually, it was never a serious relationship, so she never brought a guy home for Jackson to meet.

When Jackson was thirteen years old, Ashely met a guy, and she believed he was the type she liked. He was a good-looking guy with a good personality, reminding her of Cooper. She had an instant attraction to him. He was six feet tall with light brown hair and a thin build. His name was Seth Jacobs, and he lived in his apartment about 40 miles north of Bakersfield in Delano, California. He had a good job and made good money working late hours for UPS. He would occasionally come into the bar after delivering packages in Bakersfield. After he met her, he began going into the bar about once a week. He would have a few drinks while talking with her. His visits started becoming more frequent as their attraction to each other grew.
Once they got to know each other better, their friendship turned into a full-blown relationship.

After Seth and Ashley started dating, he would go into the bar and visit her on his time off work as often as possible. Most of the time, he would wait for her until she got off work so they could spend a little more time together. Seth sometimes drank a little too much while waiting for her. He would take her to an early morning breakfast at a restaurant that stayed open all night. On their days off, they would go to a movie or have dinner at a nice restaurant. They seemed to enjoy each other's company a great deal.

After a few months, she felt she knew him well enough to introduce him to Jackson. Before bringing him over to meet him, she sat Jackson down and talked to him about her feelings toward Seth. She told him that he was like his father, and she thought he was a nice guy. He treated her well, and they liked each other very much.

When she brought Seth over for the two to meet for the first time, Jackson felt he was nice enough. He didn't have a problem with him dating his mom, believing that if that's what she wanted, it was okay with him. In the past thirteen years since he was born, this was the first guy she had ever brought home for him to meet. He knew the guy was special to his mom, and she was serious about her relationship with him.

After that initial introduction, she brought Seth home after getting off work late at night. They would always go straight to her bedroom until the early morning hours to keep from waking Jackson. He would already be in bed sleeping, so they never bothered him when they came home together.

Seth seemed he liked Jackson and went out of his way to be friends. He decided that Jackson should learn how to drive a car just in case of an emergency. Sometimes when Ashley was busy shopping or with other things, Seth took him out into the country roads and taught him how to operate a vehicle. He was patient and even let him drive the car alone when no other traffic was on the streets. Seth felt as though it was an excellent one-on-one time between them. The two talked about many things, but it was small talk and nothing too deep. That was ok with Jackson because sometimes it was good talking to someone besides his mom. It also gave him a different perspective on life and other things.

Their relationship lasted for several months until something started happening to Seth. He and Ashley began to have a few problems in their relationship. Sometimes they would argue with each other about something, which would continue once they were back in Ashley's apartment. Sometimes their arguments got a little heated and loud, and it would wake Jackson. He tried to ignore their spats and eventually would fall back to sleep. He wouldn't say or do anything about it because he felt like it was his mom's business, and he stayed out of her personal life with men. To him, the argument sounded like she was concerned about Seth doing some drugs she didn't want him taking.

On one of those nights, they argued that it became so loud and intense it jolted Jackson straight up in his bed. Seth's tone toward Ashley was different this time than it had ever been before. Seth sounded aggressive toward her, and it sounded as though he might be getting ready to punch her or slap her around. That's when Jackson heard his mom tell Seth to get out and call an Uber to come and get him. Seth didn't listen and continued to raise his voice and argue with her.

Jackson quickly got out of bed and put on his pants and T-shirt. He sleepily walked to her bedroom door and knocked. Seth was still yelling at her as Jackson asked his mom what was going on and if everything was alright. In a frantic tone, she yelled yes and told him to return to his bedroom. She said they disagreed.

He said, "It doesn't sound like just a disagreement. It sounds more threatening to me.

Ashley said, "Everything is fine; please go back to bed."

He said, "Ok, but can you keep it down because I'm trying to sleep? You're too loud."

Respecting his mom's wishes, he slowly turned and took a step to go back to his bedroom. Seth suddenly opened the door and yelled at him in an uncontrollable rage. He was screaming in an angry and scary voice that was loud and intimidating, "Mind your own fucking business and get the fuck out of here! None of this concerns you!" Jackson was shocked because that wasn't the person he had gotten to know over the past few months. He seemed to be on some drug that altered his mental state and was out of control.

Fearing for his mom's safety, he defiantly turned back around and stood there and ignored what Seth had just said to him. Realizing that Seth was half out of his mind with anger, Jackson refused to leave the room and once again asked his mom if she was ok. Seeing that Jackson was ignoring his demand to go, Seth instantly charged at him and backhanded him across the face. The force of the blow knocked him to the floor. Once he was down on the floor, Seth pounced on his back and began to take out the anger he was feeling toward Ashley on him. Seth started to sucker punch Jackson in the face repeatedly while he lay there helpless and defenseless on his stomach. He was yelling for his mom to come and help him and get Seth off him.

She yelled at Seth to stop, and he wouldn't. She went over to him and tried to pull him off, Jackson. She reached for Seth's arm to try and pull him away, but he pushed her aside and said, "Fuck you, Ashley, get out of my face." She tried again to get him off her son, and he then backhanded her across the face and knocked her away. Seeing that he wasn't stopping his attack on Jackson, she quickly grabbed the nearest thing she could get. The heavy bottom part of a lamp was sitting on the nightstand next to her bed. As he continued to hit Jackson, almost out of reflex, she hit Seth across the side of the head as hard as possible with the lamp. He instantly fell over as though he was being shot with a rifle. Blood began to flow from his ears and nose as he dropped and lay on the floor next to Jackson. He was motionless, so Jackson slowly got up while Ashley was standing there holding the bloody lamp. She appeared in shock as she looked at him with blood running down his face from his busted eyes, nose, and lips. She said, "I'm so sorry for him doing that to you. I can't believe he went that crazy."

When he wasn't moving, Jackson bent down and felt for a pulse, but none. He looked up and said, "I think you killed him, mom. He doesn't have a pulse, and he's not breathing."

She temporarily panicked and began to cry aloud, "Oh my God, oh my God, what the hell, not again?"

He didn't know what she meant by "Not again," but calmly said, "It's ok, mom, settle down. If you hadn't pulled him off of me, he might have killed me as mad as he was and how he was punching me with his fists. I don't know what you did to piss him off, but he was completely out of control. We need to figure out what to do with his body now."

She said, "He's been doing some hard drugs lately, and that was what we were fighting over. I tried to get him to stop doing them because I feared he would overdose. It looks like it doesn't matter now."

Ashley wasn't thinking straight and didn't believe she could give the police a believable explanation about what had happened to Seth. She didn't want to get thrown in jail and held there until law enforcement figured out what happened and how he died. Ashley also didn't like the idea of the courts taking custody of Jackson while they thoroughly investigated Seth's death. Maybe they would believe her story, or perhaps they wouldn't, but she didn't want to take any chances either way. She said to Jackson, "You're right, you're right, I have to figure this out?"

She thought about things for a few minutes. She said, "We need to make Seth's death look like an accident. We should take his body back to his car and put him in it. I'll then drive his car to a spot near the Friant Kern Canal, along with one of the main roads. I'll find a place where it will be easy to run his car into the canal, and we can dump it there. I'll make sure I get out of the car before it goes into the water. You follow me in my car, and then I'll jump in with you once I'm through, and I'll drive us back to the apartment."

"I'll call the cops in the morning and tell them that I never heard from Seth after driving him back to his car at the bar. Some witnesses can collaborate that his car was at the bar and he went with me. I'll tell them he was supposed to call me when he got home, but I fell asleep and never heard from him. When the cops find the car and his body, they will probably think he fell asleep and ran off the main road and into the canal. The police will question me about everything, so we have to keep our stories straight. I'll tell them I tried to get him to stay the night because he had too much to drink, but he wouldn't listen."

Jackson said, "That sounds like a good plan, mom. I think it will work. If you want to do that, I'll back up your story with the police."

Before doing anything else, he went into the bathroom, cleaned all the blood from his nose and face, and put on a black sweatshirt and shoes.

She regained her composure and made sure nobody watched as they carried Seth's body from the apartment and put it in Ashley's car. Once they returned to Seth's car, they made sure nobody was around and transferred his body to his vehicle, just as they had planned. It was dark around three-thirty, and the air was brisk and cold. There wasn't much traffic on the roads at that time of night. Because the night and the cover of darkness helped in this situation to make their plan come together, as they went through all the plan motions, everything came out as Ashley had planned.

Once they returned to the apartment, she sat on the couch, and her body was trembling and shaking from the entire experience.

She said, "I never knew Seth to be that violent, but I think it was those crazy drugs we were fighting over. I never expected him to attack you as he did."

She had Jackson come and sit next to her for a few minutes as she put her arm around him, examined his face, and told him she loved him. And again, that she was sorry.

He said, "I love you too, mom, and none of this was your fault."

She started crying as she said, "I had fallen in love with him. It tears me up inside that he had to die like that and from my hands. I'm numb from everything that happened tonight."

He tried his best to counsel his mom but didn't know what to say. He just held onto his mom tight and tried to comfort her.

He soon got up and began taking care of the crime scene because she was too emotional and did not think about what to do next. His eyes were already starting to turn black as he cleaned up the blood from the bedroom floor and put the towels in the washing machine. He took the lamp's bottom and hid it in his secret hiding place. He would wait until he could get rid of it within the next few days.

He didn't say anything to his mom but had anger on his face and whispered, "That son of a bitch, should've kept his hands to himself. He would still be alive if he would've just backed off a little. If mom hadn't killed him, I would have eventually found a way to do it myself after what he did to me."

As she continued to sit on the couch crying, she felt terrible about killing Seth but knew she had no choice in the matter. She couldn't sit idle and let him kill her son. While reflecting on her life, she now knew why Cooper tried to keep her away from all the violent things he did to the vigilante guys. He never wanted her to feel the fear, anguish, and pain the way she was feeling at that moment. After all the years had passed, she finally understood why he kept her from everything he did.

***

Chapter 6 - Going back Home

The cruel reality of Seth's death made her understand how troubled Cooper had been in his psychopathic desire to seek revenge from the vigilante group for killing his brother. She also believed the drugs caused Seth to react as he did toward Jackson, but Cooper was never on drugs during his psychopathic rage. His problems were more deep-rooted in his family's mental history. Ashley had never seen Seth so out of control from something he was on that night. She believed he must have taken too much, and it caused him to go crazy. The police report said that the autopsy showed high doses of drugs in his system when he died.

The incident with Seth had shaken her to the bottom of her soul, bringing back all the bad memories of what happened when she killed Cooper at her mom and dad's house in Ridgecrest many years earlier. For the next week, after Seth's death, all she could think about was Cooper, Seth, and her mom telling her she hated her. Ashley longed to see her mom again despite what her mother had said so many years ago. She knew her mom loved her and wanted to sit down with her and make things right between them.

She finally realized she would never have peace of mind unless she made things right with her mom. After thinking about everything the entire week, she decided she would get Jackson to go with her and make the trip over the mountains to Ridgecrest. The bruises on his face looked healed. She wanted to see and talk to her mom and introduce Jackson to her. She believed her mom would realize he was nothing like his dad.

She tried to call her mom, but the number was out of service. She tried getting it from information, but she had no listing.

The following Monday was her day off when the two of them packed a few water bottles and headed east over the mountain pass of route 58. Jackson loved the trip because he'd never been out of Bakersfield and enjoyed the mountain scenery. He thought they were terrific and never knew they were huge, except for things he'd read. The mountains were green and lush with beautiful different-colored wildflowers along the route. He asked his mom to stop a few times to take in the fresh air and beauty of the mountains.

Once they got over the mountains, instead of turning south and going through Mojave, they turned north on route 395 and headed toward Ridgecrest. He was amazed because now the view was nothing but desert sagebrush and desert plants, and a few Joshua trees in a dry and desolate desert. He was surprised at the difference in the landscape. Everything was flush and green in the mountains, and then there was nothing but sagebrush and miles of desert plants. He laughed and said, "This place looks like a great place for jackrabbits and coyotes."

She laughed and said, "Yeah, who would ever want to live out here?"

They drove north until they came to the green sign along the road that said Red Mountain. She slowed the car down and said, "This is where your dad spent several of his younger years. Many of your relatives were buried on the property by their family but later removed by the authorities." He had never heard his family's stories but was fascinated with the history. He asked his mom if she would drive down into the heart of the little ghost town and look it over. He wanted to see the house where his dad had lived. She told him there wasn't much left because his dad burned it down when the vigilante group came looking for him and his brother. She said, "That's when they shot his twin brother, Daulton, and then he hurled himself into the fire."

He said in somewhat disbelief, "What, no way?"

"Your dad was living there the day he ran away from home. He got lost in the desert and came upon the cabin where I was being held captive. That was the day he rescued me. She just shook her head up and down because she now had tears in her eyes after telling him what happened."

She drove him by what remained of the place, and parts of the aluminum fence were still standing, but all that remained of the burned house was just ashes, charcoal, and small black pieces of burned lumber. He stared at what was left of the home and property and tried to imagine what had happened that day. He played a couple of scenarios in his mind of what he believed may have happened.

As they drove down some streets, he said, "This doesn't even look like a town. It looks almost abandoned."

She said, "That's why they call these places around here ghost towns. They've been like this for over a hundred years. They had their hey-day during the gold rush."

While driving through a few streets, she told him about going to the little bar at Randsburg, another little town about three miles away. She told him she went there with his father, and it's called "The Joint," Of course, Jackson wanted to see it as well. They had to drive over and look through the little town to see if the bar was still there. She was amazed that it was still standing, and nothing had changed since she was last there. The memories of being there with Cooper now brought tears to her eyes when she first saw the bar.

Once he was satisfied with seeing the three little ghost towns of Red Mountain, Randsburg, and Johannesburg, they returned on the highway and went north the forty miles to Ridgecrest.

When they arrived in Ridgecrest, he said, "Wow, this place is out in the middle of nowhere. It's jackrabbit land too. No wonder you didn't want to stay here."

She was suddenly serious as she said, "This town is not why I left, and you know that."

Jackson laughed and said, "I know, mom, I was just kidding with you.". I'm sure you have some good memories of this place."

She hesitated a minute and said, "You know Jackson, I never thought about it like that, but now that you mention it, I can only remember having a few good years here."

When they drove up to her mom's house, things looked different than when she last saw the place. She decided to park the car in front of the house and walk up to the front door. She told him to wait in the car until she could talk to her mom for a minute.

When she got to the front door, she knocked a few times to see if she was home. It took a few minutes, then a middle-aged woman came to the door and said, "Can I help you miss?" She told her who she was and that her mom had lived in the house the last time they had seen each other. She was now looking for her. She told the woman her mom's name.

That's when the woman slowly and carefully told her that her mom had gotten cancer three years earlier and passed away a few years ago. She said her mom had sold her and her husband the house just before she passed away. Ashley stumbled backward for a minute and thought she would pass out. The tears instantly filled her eyes and started running down her cheeks. She never expected to hear that her mom was gone, and it surprised her. When the woman saw that the news stunned her, she invited Ashley to sit for a moment and went and got her a tissue to wipe away the tears.

They sat down on the couch, and the woman said that she and her mom had conversations about her before she passed. The woman said her mom gave her a message to pass on if she ever came back home looking for her.

The woman asked, "Are you ready to hear the message from your mom?" She had written everything down on a piece of paper just in case Ashley came back.

She said, "Yes, I am ready. It took a while, but I am now."

The woman was reading from the paper, "Your mom told me to tell you that she was sorry for how she treated you and for the things she said to you the night before you left. Since she never saw you again and didn't know where you lived, she wanted me to pass this message on to you. She said she didn't mean all those hurtful things she said to you. Your mom was hurting over losing your father and took out her anger on you."

Your mom was lovely, and I'm sorry for your loss. Her gravesite is in the local cemetery next to your father's grave. Before you go to the gravesite, you should go to the funeral home because she told me there is a packet of information for you regarding her last wishes."

She thanked the woman for the information and the comforting words and asked her for directions to the funeral home.

Once she got back in the car, she put her face in her hands, broke down, and cried for a few minutes as she told Jackson what had happened to his Grandma. She felt terrible that she had been so selfish not to contact her mom all those years and let her know she was ok. She now felt like she should have told her they lived in Bakersfield, only a few hours away.

When she arrived at the funeral home, it was open, and she could go inside and talk to one of the employees who worked there. Once Ashely gave her some identification, she went to her mom's file, pulled out a sealed envelope, and gave it to her. She said, "Your mom left this for you, just in case you ever checked on her." She thanked the lady and returned to the car to meet with Jackson before opening the envelope.

When she returned to the car and opened the envelope, tons of things went through her head as she wondered what was inside. She took a few deep breaths and let them out slowly. Was her mom going to continue to chastise her and say she hated her? Are you going to say she was glad she had left or sorry for what she said? Her mind was going crazy as she took out the folded note from inside and read it slowly aloud. She immediately recognized that it was in her mom's handwriting, and the tears started to flow again.

It said what the woman that lived at her mom's house had told her earlier about how sorry she was that she had caused them to be apart from each other all those years. The letter also said that she had sold the house, her car, and everything else she owned and paid for her funeral expenses during her hospice care, including the plot next to Ashley's dad. The letter said there was $240,000 plus interest from the house's sale to go to her. It also said an Annuity would pay her $1,000 per month for the rest of her life. It said the money and Annuity contract was waiting for her in a Trust at the local Bank of America. Her mom had included the account numbers of both the bank account and the Annuity.

She was in total shock as she handed the letter to Jackson to read it for himself. She never expected anything like that from her mom because she was hoping to see her mom again and see if they could make amends and renew their love for each other again. She took a few minutes to wipe away the tears from her eyes. She was shocked by how much money her mom and dad had left for her.

Once she went to the bank and presented them with sufficient identification, she transferred the two accounts into her local bank in Bakersfield. The Annuity's monthly income had already grown by $24,000 in the past few years, which she could immediately withdraw or use when she wanted.

After completing things at the bank, they went to the cemetery and visited her mom and dad's gravesites. Once there, she bent down and spoke to her mom's grave, saying she was sorry for staying away so long and being so stubborn. She also told her mom and dad she loved them both very much. She introduced Jackson to what she believed to be their spirits resting in the graves before leaving to go back to Bakersfield.

On the drive back, he looked over at his mom and smiled as he asked, "So, mom, are we rich now?"

She smiled back and said, "No, we're not rich, but at least we can buy a little home in Bakersfield with the money, and we won't have to pay rent anymore. It will be ours, and nobody can ever kick us out. That will save us a lot of money each month, and with the Annuity money, I won't have to work as hard anymore. She yelled aloud, "Thank you, mom and dad." Jackson felt the same way as he just shook his head up and down in agreement.

When they got home, she waited a few weeks to let everything sink in and then began to search for a place she could afford with the money she had inherited from her parents. She purchased a two-story, three-bedroom condominium with an open floor plan. It had a two-car garage, and it was private because it was on its lot and had a fenced-in yard. It was in a decent neighborhood, and she only had to use about $200,000 of the money to buy it. She thought that would be the best for the two of them because there was no yard care. It was taken care of by the homeowner's association dues of $185 per month. She only had to pay the association dues and the property taxes on the property, and that was all.

Once they moved into the Condo, they believed their life was going smoothly, but the excitement and joy didn't last long because the ghosts of their past soon began to torment each of them.

***

Chapter 7 - Jackson's Independence

Not only had the Seth experience changed Ashley, but it also changed Jackson. He was thirteen and a half years old and was already five foot seven inches tall. His voice was starting to change as he began to hit puberty.

He had already killed the drug addict in the alley, which he never told his mom about, and he was involved in the cover-up of Seth's death. He no longer felt like he was the little boy that couldn't defend himself. He felt empowered to protect himself by any means possible. At that young age, he became calloused to the thought of killing someone again. He had no remorse for the men who lost their lives at the hands of him and his mother. In his distorted thinking, Jackson felt that they both deserved what they got because they tried to do to him.

As the past kept weighing heavy on her mind, Ashley started drinking too much at the bar while working. She soon abandoned the reserved attitude about not going out with the bar's patrons and started going home after work with a few of them. Ashley would often hook up with someone from the bar, stay out all night, and not return to the apartment until the next day. Jackson would get upset with her and tell her that she needed to be careful with doing that, or she might lose her job or, even worse, get hooked up with another guy like Seth. Of course, he was her son, and she still looked at him as her kid. She was the mom and felt like she could do what she wanted. She had moved from smoking pot to doing more potent and addicting drugs. She soon began doing the more popular drugs like cocaine and meth.

Her boss warned her several times about drinking on the job but didn't listen. It wasn't long before he finally had enough of her addiction and let her go from the up-scale bar and restaurant where she had worked for over ten years. The word had gotten around to the other bars about her drinking and doing drugs on the job. After that, she had a hard time finding work as a bartender.

She thought she would have to go back to waiting on tables until finally, after being out of work for about four months, she could get a job at the local dive bar called "Slim Shady's." It didn't serve food, just mixed drinks, wine, and beer. The bar was always dark inside, even during the light of the day. The owner felt like people sometimes liked to come to a dark-lit bar to drown their sorrow or whatever was ailing them. The bar had a long L-shaped wooden bar that would seat about sixteen people comfortably on wooden back bar stools. It had plenty of willing drinkers on many occasions, especially during the night hours. There were several tables with four chairs at each table, and on one side of the bar were two pool tables with Q sticks and chalk against the wall. The bar was in the rough part of town. There were always drug deals and fights in and outside the bar. The owner had to keep at least one tough bouncer on duty during open hours.

Unfortunately, her drinking problem didn't end after being fired from her last job. She stayed high most of the time while she worked and laughed and flirted with the men. She tried to convince herself that her behavior was about getting more tips but knew the truth about liking her drugs. Every time she got the chance, she would take a few drug hits to keep the high going until she got off work. The guys in the bar were always willing to give her any drugs she wanted in hopes they could take her home with them. Sometimes she would get so stoned while working that it worked.

The days of finding his mom sober became few and far between. The loneliness he was going through caused him to feel somewhat abandoned by his mother. That's when he decided to do whatever he wanted and wouldn't listen to what his mom told him. It sometimes drove him crazy to be in the same house with her and see some of the low-life guys she brought home with her.

On the first day of his second year of high school, he pretended he was going to school but ditched and never returned. During the day, he would spend time on his computer, and at night he started hanging out in places where drugs and alcohol were continually changing hands on the street.

When his mom found out he wasn't going to school, she tried her best to persuade him to go, but he no longer would listen to her about it, he had made up his mind, and he didn't want any part of the school, especially dealing with some of the bullies. To him, it represented punishment, and that's how he saw the school. He learned everything he needed on the computer. He knew his mom couldn't make him do anything he didn't want to do anymore. His attitude was more than just typical teenage rebellion because he honestly felt like he had lost his mom and felt a little lost himself.

When he started going out at night, he went to places where teenage boys and girls were hanging out. He would hide in the dark and watch the boys gather together in small groups. He would watch the boys sometimes for a few hours and try to find the ones that were the bullies that were picking on the weaker boys. Once the boys broke up from the group and went their separate ways, he would follow the bully until the opportunity was right and the boy was alone and in a dark, secluded area. He would then pull the black sock face mask down over his head and face and attack the boy. He hit the boy with his metal pipe weapon but not hard enough to kill them. He just wanted to scare them and bruise them up a little. While beating the bullies, he told them they needed to stop being a bully to the other boys, or he would come back and find them and beat them again. He mainly wanted to rough the boy enough to try and get them to stop what they were doing to the weaker boys.

He wasn't sure why he felt so angry and passionate about trying to stop them, but it was deep inside him. All he knew was that he hated how they treated the weaker victims. The way he felt about bullies was something he had reacted to since he was a young boy. It was one reason he got into so many fights and had to be transferred to many different schools when he was young. He didn't know it, but he was like that because it had been ingrained in his subconscious mind since the two young boys had tortured him when he was a baby. The other part was that he had inherited the sociopathic tendencies of his father and family members, regardless of why he took some personal pleasure in releasing his anger desires onto the bullies.

After months of beating up several bullies from different parts of the town, he started hanging out on the streets with the older drug dealers and alcoholics. He didn't want to become one of the drug runners for the drug kingpins on the drug-infested streets, so to pay for his weed, he started stealing from people's houses and selling what he stole. He didn't know it, but he soon became a "Night Crawler," just like his dad's family had been in the Red Mountain area.

During the daylight hours, he would spend his time walking from street to street until he could pick out a house he wanted to break into and steal things. Usually, the newspapers were piled on the front steps for a few days, and he felt the owners were out of town. Once he found the right house, he would find some nearby thick bushes with a good view for watching the house. He would hide behind them and watch the house and neighbors for several hours to make sure it was safe to break into the one he had picked.

After his mom left for work at night, he would use charcoal on his face and hands, wear black clothing, then go to the house and break into the place. When he did his break-in of homes, he didn't take his backpack with his weapon. Usually, the things he took were easy and quick to sell, so he took a different bag that was easy to carry.

***

Chapter 8 - Being Raped in Juvenile Detention

He was on one of his break-ins when he learned a valuable lesson about stealing from houses. It would be a lesson that would change his life forever. Unknown to him, the place he broke into had a silent alarm that went directly to the police station. Once they got the warning that he had broken into the house, the police officers were immediately dispatched to the location of the break-in. He was in the middle of the house when the police caught him red-handed.

He was arrested, went to court, and then thrown into the Juvenile Detention Center for six months. He made a promise to himself that once he got out, he would never get caught like that again. When Ashley found out what he had done, she tried to put up bail for him and did whatever she could to get him out. The judge was strict with him and decided he wouldn't let him get away with breaking into houses and stealing things. The judge hoped he would learn something and wanted to teach him a lesson, so he gave him six months in detention.

The Detention Center had sixty boys for the vast building. The bathroom area was an accessible shower area with several stalls with doors and several urinals. The floors in the shower were concrete and cold to bare feet. There were always cameras watching the inside of the enormous building, but there were no cameras in the shower area. That area was supposed to be monitored by the guards checking on it from time to time.

He soon became easy prey for bullies because he didn't have his weapon and had no friends in the Center. He was weaker and smaller than many of the center's older boys. He kept to himself because of being afraid of getting hurt by the Center's bullies. A lot of the boys were older and more brutal than him. They had lived a life of crime for a while.

The first week he was in the facility, he would cry because he missed being home with his mom after the lights went out at night. He had never been away from his mom for a long time and missed her. The loneliness and sadness he was feeling were almost overwhelming. He was careful not to let the other boys know how he felt, or they would have made his life even more miserable than they did.

One morning, he took a shower and was all lathered up with soap and ready to rinse the soap from his body. He got attacked by three inmates as they threw him against the wall and held him in place.

His eyes were stinging from the soap, and the boys took turns beating him. When they figured nobody was looking, they took turns and raped him. The attackers were two older Mexican boys and a white boy. In the area where they attacked him, the cameras couldn't see what was happening, and no guards were watching. The boys knew the guards wouldn't be watching what was happening in that area. The boys' names were Anthony Zepeda, Jonny Cantu, and Melvin Whitaker.

They were a few years older, much bigger, stronger, and meaner than Jackson. He may have been able to hold his own against just one of them but was defenseless against all three boys ganging upon him simultaneously. They picked on him because he was white, a loner, and a good-looking, blond-haired, weak-acting boy.

Even though he was embarrassed and ashamed of what happened to him, Jackson reported it to the guards. The guards ignored his complaints of being raped by the boys, so the attacks repeatedly continued while in the Center. Each time it happened, he tried to fight back but was beaten worse by the boys.

That's when he lost all respect for the law enforcement guards because they wouldn't try to help him. No matter how many times he complained about the abuse, it was only to deaf ears.

He blamed one of the guards, in particular, for allowing it to go on because he knew that Jackson was being raped and allowed it to continue. The Guard's name was Sargent Alex Santos, and he was about thirty-five years old and had an overly macho attitude. Having a stocky build and stood six foot two inches tall. Jackson had begged him to intervene and do something about what the boys were doing to him. Santos just laughed at him when he brought it up. Jackson figured that maybe the guard loved bringing agony upon the boys in the Detention Center, especially those who complained about abuse. With his attitude, he thought Santos should never have been a guard in the Center in the first place.

The last time he complained to him, Santos pulled him aside where nobody could hear him. He told him that he needed to keep his mouth shut or, even worse, things would happen to him the rest of the time he was confined there. That scared the hell out of him. He could only imagine what those worse things might be. He thought being raped by three guys was enough but didn't want to lose his life for complaining about it happening.

After that threat from Santos, he decided to keep his mouth shut. He wouldn't say anything from that point until he got out of the facility. While there, he lived in fear as he stayed frightened for his life in the Detention Center for the rest of his time. He told himself, "I'm going to keep my mouth shut for now, but they aren't going to keep me in here forever. I feel sorry for each of those boys and Sargent Santos when I get out of this fucking place." His family possessed psychopathic tendencies, and it was slowly starting to raise its ugly head as the desire for revenge had crept into his head.

For the rest of the time he was in the Center, he made it his mission to get the boys' names and addresses of where they lived. He also got the name of the town in which Sargent Santos lived. Once he had them burned in his memory, he would never forget that information. Jackson hated those four people but kept it inside, not letting anyone know his feelings. He promised himself that he would hunt each of the boys down and kill them himself once he was home and they were out of the detention facility. He was also promising to find where Santos lives, go after him, and kill him. He would be patient and wait for the boys to be released, even if it took a few years. He had memorized the dates when the courts would let each of them out of the Center.

Once he was home, he tried to talk to his mom. He wanted to tell her what had happened to him during his incarceration in the Center. He broke down and cried as he told her about all he had gone through. He told her how the three boys held him against his will and raped him repeatedly while in there. He said that he didn't have any friends in the Center to help protect him, and the guards just let it keep happening. He told her he complained to the Guards about the abuse a few times until the main guard threatened him for speaking up about being raped.

The entire time he told his mom about what happened to him, she sat across from him and just cried as he told her. It broke her heart, and she said, "I'm sorry, I tried everything I could to get you out of that place, but the Judge wouldn't listen. He kept saying he wanted you to learn a valuable lesson, and maybe you wouldn't break into houses anymore." He told his mom she should've tried harder because he would never get over what those people did to him there.

A few nights later, when she was high on drugs and lounging on the couch at home, she decided to talk to him about what he had told her again. She was in a drunken stupor as she stumbled into his room and sat on his bed. She wanted to tell him how she felt about everything he told her.

She pointed at Jackson and said that he had brought all of what happened to him upon himself. She noted that it was all his fault because he broke the law when breaking into the houses. She told him that he shouldn't have been out there breaking into homes and stealing things in the first place. He just sat there and listened as the tears well up in his eyes and began rolling down his cheeks. She couldn't have hurt him any worse if she had stabbed him in the heart with a dagger.

He looked her in the face and said, "I can't believe you can say something like that. Nobody should ever be beaten up, held against their will, and raped, especially by three guys. I hate you for saying that to me. You can leave my room now that I know how you feel."

She stood up, stumbled out of his room, and went to her bedroom.

After hearing her saying those hurtful things to him, he believed she was consumed in her own life with drugs and alcohol that she'd given up on him. He no longer had the one person to turn to for desperately needed support and comfort. He felt empty and deserted inside and accepted the belief that he was all alone in the world and that nobody cared if he lived or died.

***

Chapter 9 - Jackson's Revenge

As Jackson sat home while his mom worked nights, he had flashbacks of what happened during his incarceration at the Detention Center. He had difficulty coping with reality. He was confused why the boys had done that to him because of his experience. He didn't do anything to the three boys to deserve what they did to him. He wondered why they felt compelled to pick him out of all the other boys in the facility and raped him repeatedly. He thought, "Maybe it was because of being smaller than them and appearing weak and unable to defend me against the three of them. Maybe it was because he was a loner and didn't want anything to do with the other boys. Maybe he was just an easy target, or maybe his mom was right, and he deserved it." He didn't know the answer but became obsessed with why the abuse had happened to him. It began to torment him day after day. He couldn't think of anything else but what he had gone through. He became overwhelmed with self-guilt, shame, and self-pity because of the rape.

He was having trouble going out at night and breaking into houses as he had done before. He knew he had to do something about his feelings, or he would be full of self-doubt and anger for the rest of his life. He also knew that he would be confined to his home indefinitely if he didn't do something to get even with what they had done to him.

He was preoccupied with his issues but couldn't shake the feeling of hatred toward the boys and the guard. He blamed the guard as much as he blamed the boys for what had happened to him. It was as though he possessed some innate obsession or desire for revenge and had no control over his anger or emotions. He knew that if his dad were alive, he wouldn't let the boys and the guard go unpunished for their unspeakable abuse against him. He also knew that if his mom weren't addicted to drugs and in her right mind, she wouldn't have let them get away with it. He knew she would've been fighting with the Judge to get him out of that place if she knew what he was going through. But now, he had neither of them to help and was all alone.

After what his mom had said to him about deserving what he got, his heart became hardened and calloused in a way that he would never be able to explain or overcome. His anger consumed his every thought, both night and day.

He used the computer, extensively researched law enforcement files, and searched for Cooper's father's files. He found out about his father's deep-rooted desire to get revenge against the individuals of a local vigilante group that had killed his twin brother, Dalton. He believed he understood because he felt the same deep passion for revenge toward the boys and the detention center guard as his dad did against that group of men.

He also found out that his mom was the one that had killed his dad, and it happened at her mom and dad's house. The report said she was afraid for herself and her mom and dad's lives, which was why she killed him. It said she killed him in self-defense, but she shot him point-blank in the heart. Now he understood why she had said, "Not Again," the night she killed Seth.

It bothered him, and he wanted to know what happened and why she killed his father. The next day he confronted his mom about it. He wanted to know precisely how and why she killed someone she was supposed to love by shooting him in the heart.

When he first asked her about it, she was shocked and said, "Where did you get that information?" Tears immediately filled her eyes.

He replied, "I found it on the computer when I looked up my dad's police report."

Ashley slowly collected her thoughts and carefully said, "The day I killed him, your dad came to our house in a panic after thinking he had killed a highway police officer on the main road heading into Ridgecrest. Your dad rushed into our home and quickly shut the door. He was waving his gun around as if he were going to kill us. My dad thought he was there to harm us, so he grabbed my mom's gun and aimed it at my dad. While he did that, my mom called the police and told them Cooper was the one that shot the police officer and that he was at our house threatening everyone. Your dad kept saying he would kill my father if he didn't quit aiming the gun at him and telling him to put it down. I couldn't get your dad to put his weapon down because he was waiting for the police to come and get him, and he would kill more officers.

My dad took a wild shot at your dad, who missed him, and things started to spiral out of control. I thought your dad was going to kill us all, so when he had his back turned from us looking out the window for approaching police, I took the gun from my dad, and I went up to your dad and put one arm around him and hugged him and one behind me. I held the gun in my other hand, and when I couldn't get him to calm down, I shot him in the heart. So there, you have it, and yes, I did love your dad with all my heart and soul, but I wasn't going to let him kill my entire family."

He accepted her explanation and understood why she did what she had done. He could tell by the tears rolling down her face as she told the story that it still hurt her to relive things. He knew it still weighed heavy on her heart.

He continued his extensive research and found out where Sargent Santos lived. He figured how much time it would take to use his bicycle, ride near the Sargent's home, and back again after completing his task. Once his plan was formulated, he started taking steps for his first attack. Sargent Santos was the first one on his list to kill.

In his preparations, he first found a home he believed the owners might possess firearms. He decided that he would be wiser now than on the previous break-in, so he picked a house that didn't show any signs of alarms. When he found the perfect place for him, he waited until around midnight and broke into the house. He then went and stayed hidden in the bushes for thirty minutes to make sure the police didn't show up to arrest him again after a silent alarm. Once he felt comfortable, he made his way through the house, looking for places where someone may hide a gun.

After several minutes of searching, he found a 38 pistol with a box of shells next to it on the nightstand. It was by the bed in the Master Bedroom and next to the bed. Not wanting to bring any additional suspension to himself that may alert police for breaking into a house, he quickly left once he had the gun. He then went back to his house, carefully put the gun and the ammunition in a folded towel, and put it in a hiding place his mom didn't know where.

The next night when his mom left to go to work, he took the gun and ammunition out and carefully looked it over. He made sure the firing pin was in place, and no parts were missing from the weapon. Once he felt comfortable, he stuck it in his backpack and rode his bike to a vacant field several blocks away. When he was sure nobody else was around, he took the gun out and loaded it with a few live rounds. He then cocked the gun and took the safety off, and fired a shot in the air. At first, it stunned him with the loud noise it made, especially in the middle of the night and away from the city's noise.

Once he knew the gun would fire, he quickly ejected the other rounds, put them back in his backpack, and jumped on his bike. He rode as fast as he could to get out of the area. He knew it wouldn't be long before the police would be driving by and looking for the person that fired the shot.

After he got back home, he did the same thing as before and took the gun and hid it in his secret hiding place. Soon he would be ready to go after his first person of revenge.

The next night Jackson put a black sock cap on his head to cover his blond hair and wore a black hooded sweatshirt. He took his time and made it several miles to the neighborhood and home of Sargent Santos. Once he was on the street, he became highly vigilant in exploring the entire subdivision and how easy or hard it would be to escape once he accomplished his goal.

As he carefully checked out the surrounding houses, he noticed a lot of activity in the street. A group of teenagers was hanging out just a few doors from Santos' home. They played basketball in the street with one of those moveable basketball nets.

He also observed Sargent Santos' house and another house down the street with outside exterior cameras to take videos. It covered the front yard and out into the middle of the cul-de-sac. Santos's house was close to the end of the street, and getting out of the subdivision fast without being caught would be extremely difficult.

Once he got home, he thought about it and decided to try a different location for Santos' plan to kill. He knew that if he made one mistake, it could cost him his life or, even worse, his freedom for the rest of his life. He swore to himself he would never be incarcerated again. He knew they had cameras surrounding the Juvenile Detention Center's entire compound, so he couldn't do it there. While he was thinking about everything, he remembered Sargent Santos bragging to the other guards about his bowling. He told them he was in a bowling league that bowled every Thursday night with the guys from 7 to 10. He would bowl at the bowling alley on Wible Road.

The next day he rode his bike to the bowling alley and checked things out for himself. After feeling comfortable with this location, Jackson had to try and catch Sargent Santos before he went into the bowling alley or came out alone. At 7 pm, it was already dark that time of year, so he could wear black clothing and stay hidden while waiting to make his move. Jackson picked a location near the building with tall bushes and trees to watch the parking lot. He found an open area behind the bushes to hide his bike and stay invisible while he observed everything from there.

He went inside and pretended that he wanted to come and bowl on Thursday night as he asked the person working behind the counter if they still had any open bowling on Thursday night. She told him that most of the lanes would be used by the league bowlers on Thursday night and that another night may be better for him to come and bowl. He thanked her for her information and then had the information he needed.

For the next few weeks, he visited the bowling alley around 6:30 at night and waited to see if he could get a look at Sargent Santos coming and going from the bowling alley. He was just like clockwork as he showed up right on time every Thursday night. Santos parked his new pick-up near the middle of the parking lot and away from the other vehicles because he didn't want anyone opening up their doors and putting dents in his new truck.

When he first sees Sargent Santos again, he has difficulty controlling his anger and hatred for him. He wanted to rush out and immediately confront Santos and kill him but calmed himself down as he told himself to be patient.

He found that many of the bowlers would simultaneously get to the bowling alley. That would make it difficult for him to attack when Santos first arrived. He
found that many bowlers had a few beers while bowling before getting in their vehicles to leave. He saw that Santos always stayed a little longer than the other bowlers and had a few more beers while talking to one of the female servers before leaving alone.

The following Thursday, Jackson put everything together to carry out his attack. He had the loaded gun in his backpack with extra ammunition as he went to his hiding place at the bowling alley. He was so nervous from the anticipation of the attack that he had gotten there early and waited. The night was dark, and it seemed extra quiet on this night. Maybe it was the same as before, but Jackson had been so preoccupied with his thoughts that he never noticed how slow it was in the parking lot. While waiting, he kept whispering and telling himself to settle down and not lose his concentration and focus. Sargent Santos was right on time, so Jackson began to go over precisely what he would do when he came out of the bowling alley.

Sargent Santos didn't disappoint him as he lingered inside and had a couple of extra beers as he had done before. While waiting for him to come out, he was getting impatient as he whispered, "Come on, man, get your ass out here where I can kill you." When he saw him coming out of the bowling alley, he quickly took the gun out of his backpack and took the safety off, so it was ready to fire. He pulled the sock cap down over his hair and zipped up his black hooded sweatshirt.

Santos had consumed too many beers and wasn't walking in a straight line. He staggard toward his vehicle as he looked down at the keys in his hand. Jackson jumped on his bike and went not too far behind Santos. He pretended to make loops in the parking lot with his bicycle to get close to Sargent Santos. Santos was so intoxicated that he didn't even notice what Jackson was doing.

When he reached his vehicle, Santos momentarily stopped and fumbled for the right key on his ring of keys to start his truck. Just as he clumsily got inside his truck and reached to shut the door, Jackson was there and held the door open with his body as he put the gun to Sargent Santos's head, and just before he pulled the trigger, he said, "Hey motherfucker, do you remember me? You let those three boys keep raping me in the Center and didn't stop them." Santos had a wide-eyed look on his face as he stared momentarily into his face. He started to reach for his gun, and Jackson immediately pulled the trigger. Blood and brain matter splattered on the window on the other side of the truck. He was careful not to touch anything with his hands to leave any fingerprints as he kicked the door shut behind him with his knee once Santos was dead.

Right after he shot him, he took off at full speed on his bike into the dark part of the parking lot. He used an escape route away from the murder scene mapped out days before. When he got back on the street about a mile away, he began to hear the first sirens blasting in the silence of the night as the police headed to the scene of his crime.

On the way home, he said, "You should've tried to help me, you fucking asshole. You didn't have to let those three fuckers continue raping me. You got what you deserved."

When he got home, he cleaned the prints off the gun and hid them in his hiding place. He was proud of himself as he sat down on the edge of the bed and looked at himself in his mirror. He smiled and said, "That's one. Three more to go."

The next day, after he awoke, he took the gun from its hiding place, used a hammer, and broke it into several pieces. Once he had a handful of metal parts, he began to go up and down the central part of the town and dropped parts of the gun into trash dumpsters at different locations. He decided to lay low for a few months before he started going out again at night.

***

Chapter 10 - Going after Cantu

It had been a month, and Jackson began to feel comfortable about being safe from the authorities coming to his apartment and questioning him regarding Sargent Santos' death. While in the Detention Center, he had complained to the Judge about the three boys repeatedly raping him. He also complained about the Guards' lack of protection.

He thought someone from the law enforcement department would have a few questions. For those reasons, he kept waiting to see if someone would show up the entire time he was home, but it never happened. Each day at home, he realized he could kill someone and escape murder. He began to gain more and more pride and confidence in himself for his act of revenge. During this time, he had just turned fourteen, killed two people, and helped his mom with the third.

About two months after he killed Santos, he started going out to his familiar locations and touching base with some of the savory characters he'd gotten to know the past few years. After hanging out for several days, he felt comfortable with being out on the streets again at night. He went back to smoking pot and drinking a few beers while on his own.

A few months later, he hung out on the streets and went from one location to another. He almost stopped in his tracks when he saw a familiar person he could never forget. One of the thugs who had beaten him and repeatedly raped him in the Detention Center was Johnny Cantu. He wasn't supposed to get out of the Center for another five months, but he figured they let him out early. He was another guy about his exact age, but it wasn't Anthony Zepeda or Melvin Whitaker.

When he first saw Cantu, he stiffened in anger as rage temporarily took control of his body. The pain from his horrible experiences with Cantu almost overwhelmed him for a brief moment. He wanted to go over to him and put a bullet in his head, but he didn't. He could feel the blood rush to his face as the anger almost gave away to reasoning as he watched one of his most hated assailants.

He wasn't ready to encounter Cantu then, but he wanted to get revenge against him. Cantu was seventeen, but he wasn't driving a car. He was on foot. Jackson immediately took his bike, ducked into the darkness, and hid in a few tall, thick bushes along the street. He was hoping Cantu didn't recognize him, so he stayed hidden from him. Afraid that if he did recognize him, he might quickly leave and not be able to follow him and see where he lived. He watched every move Cantu and his friend made. He hid his bike behind some tall bushes and then followed them on foot wherever they went. He soon found that they were trying to contact one of the drug dealers to hit on drugs.

Once the two guys made their drug deal, they immediately started heading to another location to do their private drugs, not on the street. It was dark, but he could follow them from a distance. There was a full moon out, but they never noticed he had followed them to an abandoned commercial building not far away. They were more concerned about getting to where they were going and doing their drugs than worrying about someone behind them.

Once at the building, they met up with a few other guys already there. They were sitting around a fire they had built in the middle of the room and doing their drugs. Jackson had made his way up to the opposite end of the building and carefully peeked through a broken and partially missing window as he stayed hidden and watched them for a few hours. He stayed ducted down in a crouched position and occasionally raised to see if they were still there.

He watched until Johnny decided to leave the group, and when he did, he was left alone. He walked along the street for several blocks, and Jackson followed him again. Cantu went to an older part of town where many low-income people lived. He watched as Cantu went to a run-down shack of a house. There was a light on in the front, and Jackson watched until he disappeared inside and turned off the light.

He whispered, "Now I see why he didn't like me and wanted to punish and torture me. He was jealous of me and probably thought I was just a rich kid that got in trouble. It didn't give him a free pass to do what he did to me."

Once he had the address and knew where Cantu lived, he turned and was careful not to let anybody see him as he left. Every time a car would pass by, he would duck into a dark area to stay hidden, making his way back toward the central part of town. He then picked up his bike and rode back to his apartment. Once home began to formulate a plan to get his revenge against Cantu. He went over a few different scenarios as to what the best way would be to kill him.

He put his weapon, charcoal, a black sock cap, duct tape, and a sharp knife in his backpack and went out night after night, hoping to run into Cantu again. He did that for about two months until he finally saw him again with his same friend. Jackson did the same thing he had done before, stashed his bike and followed him. It was dark out this night because there was no moon at all.

He watched them again for a few hours, and when he saw the guys were breaking up their meeting, he quickly left ahead of him and took the same path that Cantu had taken before on his way home. He found a few large bushes on the same side of the sidewalk that Cantu would have to pass and hid in them. It wasn't too far from Cantu's home. He put the charcoal on his face and hands and the sock cap over his head. When he saw him coming down the path, he quickly pulled his metal weapon from his backpack, wrapped his hand through the handle, and held it tight. He looked around to see if anyone had been watching or following him or Johnny. His heart was pounding fast and loud, and the closer Cantu got, the faster and louder it seemed to beat and sound.

Just as Cantu passed by where he was hiding, he was checking something on his phone. Jackson jumped out from behind him and immediately hit him in the side of the head with his metal weapon. He instantly fell to the sidewalk, and Jackson hit him a couple more times with the pipe to make sure he was unconscious. Quickly pulling the duct tape from his backpack, and put a strip across Cantu's mouth. He then pulled down his pants and underwear, grabbed his penis and balls in his left hand, took the sharp knife from his backpack, and quickly cut everything off. The blade cut through his skin with ease. He stuck the penis and testicles in a plastic bag, pulled the duct tape from Cantu's mouth, and put everything back in his backpack.

Blood was spurting everywhere as he turned and left. He began to run as Cantu started waking up from being knocked unconscious. Jackson had gotten only a few blocks away when he first heard his victim's faint and painful screams. Cantu was shocked, squirming around on the sidewalk, trying to see what had happened to him. He reached down to his crotch and found nothing but the blood that filled his hand. Jackson smiled because he knew it would be just a short time, and Cantu would bleed.

He returned to where he had stashed his bike and then headed home. He heard the ambulance and police's faint sirens, and the sound got louder as they got closer and headed in Cantu's direction. Jackson dumped Cantu's penis and testicles from the plastic bag into a large trash bin on his way home. He also stopped at a house where a water hose was lying out front, and he could wash off his knife and hands.

He thought the night was peaceful and calm, away from the scene, and he enjoyed his ride back home. Once home, he sat on the edge of the bed, smiled, and whispered, "That's two! That fucker got what he deserved."

A few days later, he was back on his computer and searched police records to see if he could find anything on Anthony Zepeda and Melvin Whitaker. He soon found that each of them still had several months to spend in the Juvenile Detention Center before they were letting them out. Seeing that, he decided to lay low until it got closer to their release date. He would go out three or four nights a week during that time and roam the streets and break into a few houses.

***

Chapter 11 - Ashley and Jackson's strained Relationship

Several weeks after they had their first talk, it was Ashley's day off work. Jackson was in his room on the computer when she knocked on his door and asked if she could come in and talk with him. His mom was waisted during their last conversation and had said some hurtful and awful things to him. She hoped he would listen to her apology and forgive her for those things she said. She had been feeling terrible about them for some time and wanted to see if they could make amends with each other.

When she asked him if she could talk to him, he reluctantly said, "Ok, but what about?"

At first, she wasn't sure exactly what to say as she sheepishly approached him and sat on the edge of his bed across from where he was sitting at the computer. He turned his chair around to face her. He was standoffish and a little apprehensive about having a conversion with her because he wasn't sure if she was now stoned or sober.

He pushed his chair back away from the desk and defiantly crossed his arms as he said, "So what do you want to say now? I need to be back in the Detention Center to get raped again?" He still felt the sting of the words she had said to him during their last conversation about deserving what he got. He knew she was stoned when she said those things to him but didn't it give her the right or excuse to say those horrible things to him?

She had tears in her eyes as she said, "God no, Jackson, that is the last place I want you to be. I was wrong for saying those horrible things to you before, and I'm sorry from the bottom of my heart. I know my words hurt you, and I hope you can forgive me for saying you deserved your pain. You didn't deserve what those boys did to you, and I had no right to say that you deserved what they did. Nobody would ever deserve that. I've been thinking about it, and I treated you the way my mom treated me when I left and never went back. I wouldn't blame you if you never wanted to speak to me or have anything to do with me again, but I'm asking you to forgive my stupidity."

He thought, "Man if she only knew that I killed that sorry guard Santos that let me get raped repeatedly and killed one of the rapists when I cut off his penis and testicles, she probably wouldn't be apologizing to me right now. She'd probably want to take me to the facility and check me there."

Then she said something that surprised him and made him realize how sincere she was in her apology. She said, "You know, Jackson, if you want to go after the guys that raped you when they get out, I can help you with that. I've been thinking about it, and it's been driving me crazy that they did that to you. I wish I could kill them myself. That's one reason I've been getting drunk so much since you were in that place. Ever since you told me what they were doing to you there, and I couldn't get the judge to budge in his decision, I've had a hard time living with myself. If your dad were alive, he wouldn't let those boys get away with what they did. He would probably kill them or, at the very least, help you kill them."

He unfolded his arms and wrapped his arms around her as she began to sob. He said, "It's ok, mom. I'm almost grown now, and I can take care of myself. I don't need you to get involved with any of my acts of revenge." He rolled his eyes while hugging her and said, "If I were to decide to do something to them, it would be on me and not you. I wouldn't want you to get in trouble by helping me break the law in any way."

She said, "Your dad said those same words to me when he went after some of the vigilante guys when I offered to help him."

He said, "Maybe my dad and I are more alike than you know or would ever like to admit."

He told her that she needed to support him no matter what he did. He said, "You're my mom and the only person in this world that loves me, and you are the only person in this world that I love, so we need to be there for each other, even if one of us kills someone. Like you did when you accidentally killed Seth. I was there for you, and I had your back if the police would've come after you for his death. If I were to kill one of the guys that raped me, you need to be there for me, especially if I got caught. Please don't ever say hurtful things like that or abandon me again. This world is lonely without you and I being there for each other."

She stopped sobbing, wiped away the tears, and said, "You're right. I need to be a better mom. I know it's no excuse, but I was pretty fucked up the last time I hurt you so deeply with my words. I know how deeply words can hurt because of what my mom said when I left. I promise I will never do that or abandon you like that again. If you decide to take revenge against those boys, I will do whatever you ask me to help you get even with them.   I can't help but worry about you being out on the streets late at night and alone. If you're going to be alone at night and do something against the law, then make sure you don't get caught."

He told her that he had become very independent in the past few years and learned to protect himself in the streets. He told her he could care for himself even in the roughest parts of town at night. He said, "I will never let someone rape me again. I promise you that I will kill them first."

He was relieved and happy to hear his mom say she was sorry for the hurtful things she had said to him during their last conversation. After saying she would help him if he wanted revenge against the boys, he felt like she had his back again. He now believed his mom would support him once again no matter what he may do. Although he felt better about their relationship, he wouldn't let her know what he was about to do to the remaining rapists in the future. He thought some things were better left unsaid, and she didn't need to know about them.

***

Chapter 12 - Going after Anthony Zepeda

He spent the next several days on the computer trying to find Zepeda and Whitaker's status and when they might get released from the Detention Center. He found out that Zepeda would be the next person discharged from the Center, and it would be sometime within the next few months. He also found out that Melvin Whitaker still had time to do after Zepeda was released. Once he had that information, he knew his next target: Zepeda.

He still remembered the address of where Zepeda lived before he went into the Detention Center. He found out it was near one of the worst areas of south/east Bakersfield off Baker Street and was surprised that it was only about six miles south of where he lived. He would have to be careful while in that area at night because there was a lot of crime. The guys on the street told him to stay out of that area, especially at night.

He couldn't help himself. He felt compelled to go after Zepeda. Even if it meant going to his home, he thought he had everything needed to start being vigilant and ready to make his next attack. He began planning how he was going to try and kill Zepeda.

All he could think about during the day was how much he hated Zepeda for what he had done to him in the Center. He became obsessed with it as he planned out many different ideas of what he wanted to do to him. He believed that where Zepeda lived would have a lot to do with how and when he carried out his plan.

One night he was so impatient that he went against all the warnings and decided to go to the area where Zepeda lived and check it out for himself. He put on his backpack with all his protective items inside and headed to the neighborhood. It was dark and creepy, just like the guys on the street said it was. When he arrived in the area, he could hear police sirens blaring in the distance and occasional sporadic gunfire from somewhere in the neighborhood.

The place gave him chills, and he felt like the hair on the back of his neck was standing up as he found the street and address of Zepeda. Even though it was late at night, people still walked the streets. He felt like this was the creepiest place he'd ever been to, almost like being in a slow-motion horror film. From the looks and sounds of the area, he didn't think he would have time to pull off an attack on Zepeda near his home. While watching the place, his instincts told him that he'd have to devise another way to kill Zepeda. He felt he could've gotten killed before getting out of that area.

As he made his way out of the area, he went down one of the streets, and a huge black African American man approached him from behind. He grabbed him by his arm and held him in place. He held onto Jackson and asked him what he was doing in that area and alone at that time of night. He had an angry look on his face and was huge and mean-looking.

He quickly lied and told him he was looking for a friend from school. The guy asked him what his friend's name was, and Jackson made up a fake name of Richard Sandoval.

The guy looked him in the face and said, "I've never heard of him. Are you sure he lives in this neighborhood?"

He quickly said, "Maybe I wrote the address wrong, but I was sure he told me it was somewhere around." The guy let go of his arm and said, "Look, kid, I'm going to do you a life-saving favor. I don't know if your friend lives in this area, but you need to get out of here as quickly as possible. Don't you know this is a dangerous place for a white person, especially at night? The people here would just as soon kill you as look at you."

His words shook him to the bone as shivers temporarily went up his back. He thanked the guy and told him he was getting out of there as quickly as possible. He began to jog away from the guy, heading back the way he'd come.

At that moment, he didn't think getting revenge on Zepeda meant much if he got killed. He would have to go back home and plan more on getting him out in the open and away from his house and neighborhood. He wasn't sure how but knew he couldn't go back into that neighborhood and kill him there after receiving the warning.

As he lay on his bed later that night, he looked at the bruises on his arm and thought, "That guy had such a strong grip on my arm it was like it was in a vice. I'm lucky he wasn't one of the bad guys who wanted to kill me because I was white. I need to be a little more careful in the future and not trust everyone I encounter. I wouldn't have had time to get my weapon out before that guy could've broken me in half. I'm just lucky. I think that guy may have saved my life."

As he thought about things, he understood why Zepeda was so screwed up. He believed if anyone lived in an area like that, they might be afraid to come out of their house at night. He whispered, "Just because of where he lived or how he grew up didn't give him the right to attack me in the Center and rape me repeatedly." He wouldn't give him a free pass because of where he lived.

His mind hadn't changed regarding his Zepeda. He couldn't get rid of the hatred he had for him. He kept thinking about what he might do to kill him if he could somehow draw him out in the open. He finally had formulated a plan but would need a couple of guns to carry it out and protect himself if something went wrong. He knew the only way to get them was to break into a few houses until he found what he was after.

For the next few weeks, he took his time and broke into several houses until he found a couple of pistols and plenty of ammunition he could stuff into his backpack and have with him to carry out his plan.

On the day Zepeda was supposed to get out of the Detention Center, he got up early and made his way to the Center. He hid in a treed area a few blocks away as he waited and watched. He was about to give up when an older light green chevy car parked in the front. A middle-aged man got out and went up to the building. He rang the outside bell and was let inside by the guards. After about fifteen minutes, Zepeda came walking out carrying a white plastic bag with his things inside and the older gentleman walking along beside him. As they got into the car, Jackson was bursting with all kinds of angry emotions. He wanted so much to pull out one of the guns, go up to him, and put a bullet in his head, just like what he'd done to Sargent Santos.

He had learned from the Center that they had cameras pointed in all directions and knew he'd get caught. They would've seen him commit the killing. He knew that if he did that, he'd been right back in that place once again. He could feel the blood rush to his face, and his muscles stiffened with anger as he watched them drive away. He whispered through gritted teeth, "Your days on this Earth are numbered, Zepeda. You better enjoy your newfound freedom while you're still alive." He then returned to his house to rest, relax, and think about his next move.

He knew Zepeda would be back on the streets soon because he'd heard him talk about being there when he was in the Center. Jackson initially thought about starting a war between rival gangs when Zepeda was in the town where the gang members hung out. He thought he could get near Zepeda and fire off several rounds in the direction of one of the gang members; as Zepeda walked near, they would think it was him firing at them. Then they would go after him and kill him. That plan had a problem because it would be too easy for things to backfire, and the gang would come after him instead of Zepeda. His instincts, once again, told him that idea was a little too risky to try and pull off. He probably would've ended up getting killed himself trying that plan.

He spent some time in the drug trafficking area, where gang members would occasionally come and go to get their drugs. They sometimes would get into gun battles when a rival gang would show up simultaneously as the other one. Sometimes killings would take place during their confrontations. He began to hang out there to see if Zepeda would show up and wait for one gang member to kill another rival.

He found out about a recent killing of a gang member and took a chance with that window of opportunity. He anonymously slipped a note to the rival gang of the guy killed, and the letter said that Anthony Zepeda was the guy who killed their friend. The message gave them his address where they could find him.

The gang members did a drive-by shooting within the next few days after delivering the note to the member. They waited until Zepeda left his house and killed him in the front yard.

Once he learned about the killing, Jackson smiled and said, "Alright, my plan worked. That's three!"

He waited for about a month before he did any research regarding Melvin Whitaker. He then went through the same process to get information on him as he had done to get Zepeda's information. He couldn't believe it when he read the latest report on Whitaker. He had mixed emotions of happiness and disappointment when he discovered that Whitaker had been killed at the Detention Center by two inmates. The report said that he had been wrapped in a blanket while sleeping. He had been beaten with some blunt object by the inmates. One of the inmates had pushed a long screwdriver from under his chin and into his brain. It killed him instantly.

Jackson believed he knew what had happened between him and the two inmates who killed him. He thought that Zepeda, Cantu, and Whitaker had rapped the two inmates repeatedly, as they had done with him. When Zepeda and Cantu were released, Whitaker didn't have protection from them and was the only one left of the three rapists. He became an easy target for the two boys, and the shoe was then on the other foot. He could no longer defend himself from the two inmates. They probably got tired of complaining to the guards about being assaulted and raped and not getting any results. Rather than let it continue, the inmates decided to do something about it themselves and took the law into their own hands. If that's what happened, he understood how the inmates felt. If he had someone to back him up and help him, maybe he would've done the same thing when he was in there.

He then kicked back on his bed and whispered, "Well, it's too bad I couldn't have taken Whitaker out myself, but it's all good. That's four and the end of my agonizing and torturous revenge at the Center."

He thought, "IF ONLY I could tell my mom that all four people responsible for beating me and raping me at the Center are now dead."

***

Chapter 13 - Ashley's Assaulted

He wanted to stay home for a few months and reflect on the past few years. He tried to think about what he'd been through and wanted to find a way to forget everything. He was fifteen and had been through far more than the average adult would ever imagine. His mom was busy with her work and occasionally doing drugs. She wasn't doing as much as he had done in the past but still enjoyed getting high.

When they were both homes, they didn't talk much with each other. It was mostly just small talk when they did sit down together. Jackson felt it was as if one of them didn't want to know what the other was doing in their lives. It was as though they were afraid to find out because they would have to talk about it and face the demons. There wasn't much hugging between the two, mainly because Jackson was at the age where he got embarrassed for showing his mom affection.

She worked late most nights at the bar, but after hours on Friday and Saturday nights would go with some of the regulars from the bar to her boyfriend, Sam Freeman's house. He was her new boyfriend, and he had long brown hair, a mustache, a goatee, and a slim build. Sam was a nice guy with a good personality, and everyone liked him. He worked in construction during the day but enjoyed his drugs and alcohol a little, too, much like Ashley. Especially on the weekends when he didn't have to work the next day. A group of people would meet at his house and party with each other until the early morning hours. They got high by smoking pot, doing recreational drugs, and drinking alcohol. Most of the time, everyone was mellow and just sitting around talking with each other and getting high. They laughed and told stories and sometimes talked about current events on the news.

She and Sam had been hanging out with each other for several months, and Jackson had met him but never told his mom if he liked him. He felt it was her business who she wanted to have as a boyfriend. Being a loner, Jackson didn't like the group concept of smoking pot with someone else, thinking it was a little bizarre. He knew that sometimes when people smoke weed or do drugs, they react in strange ways, like the guy that chased him down the street and he ended up killing. Jackson always believed he was high on something, and that was why he chased after him.

On one of those Saturday nights, Sam and Ashley were kicking back on the couch after she got off work. They were doing some drugs with their friends at Sam's house. It was around three in the morning, and everyone had left the house except Sam and Ashley. At least, they thought everyone had left as they sat next to each other on the couch and took a bit more drugs together.

Sean Thomas was a friend of a few other people who occasionally showed up at Sam's house during the after-hour parties. Sam and Ashley didn't know him very well but had smoked weed with him a few times when he was there. He was good-looking, around six feet tall, with black hair and blue eyes. He seemed like a nice guy to Sam, and his other friends said he was nice. Ashley thought it was strange that a good-looking guy like him never brought a girl over with him to their parties.

He began to creep her out the more times she was around him. He had his eye on her when she moved from one room to the other or sat on the couch next to Sam. She also told Sam that Sean tried to flirt with her when Sam wasn't looking. He wasn't subtle in his teasing, and that bugged her. Sean didn't respect Sam or care what Sam may say or think about his flirting with Ashley. She didn't like being around him because he always made her uncomfortable when he showed up at the after-hours party.

This night, she wore a tight light blue blouse and a short white skirt. She had let her hair down and was looking exceptionally sexy. Sean couldn't keep his eyes off her as he watched her every move.

Once alone, Sam and Ashley were getting pretty stoned on the couch. As everyone had left Sam's house, Sean had hidden in one of the bedrooms until everyone else was gone. He watched and waited until the two passed out next to each other on the couch before he approached them. Ashley was lying with her skirt pulled up to mid-thigh, and her light pink panties were showing. She wasn't wrapped in Sam's arms but lying next to him.

Seeing her in that vulnerable position was too much temptation for Sean. He always wanted to get her in bed and figured now would be the perfect opportunity for him. He believed she was so waisted from the drugs she wouldn't even know that he carried her to the bedroom and made love to her.

He slowly crept over to the couch and carefully picked her up in his arms, ensuring Sam didn't wake up. Sean figured if Sam woke up when he picked her up, he would tell him he was helping her to bed. He carried her toward the spare bedroom, and she slightly woke up but didn't open her eyes. She believed Sam was taking her to bed as she said, "Sam, I'm so sleepy," and then passed out again. He didn't say anything as he continued to the spare bedroom.

He closed the door with his leg and laid her on her back in the bed. She moved around slightly as if to get comfortable. Then, Sean slowly took her skirt and panties off and laid them on the nightstand next to the bed. He left her top because it would've been too hard to take off, and he didn't want to wake her.

Once she was partially nude, he returned to the door and peeked out to ensure Sam was still on the couch. Seeing Sam sleeping, he took off all his shoes, pants, and underwear and laid them next to the bed. Sean crawled onto the bed and then carefully began to penetrate her and go through the motions of sex. While he was on top of her, she began to wake up and realized something was wrong.

Realizing it wasn't Sam, she yelled, "What the fuck, what are you doing? Get off of me, mother fucker." It was dark in the room, and she didn't know who was on top of her, but she knew it wasn't Sam. Sean then hit her in the chin and the face with his closed fist and knocked her out. He jumped off of her and put his pants and shoes on. He ran out of the house and left as quickly as possible.

She woke up a few minutes later and started screaming. Sam heard her screams and clumsily made his way to the hallway. He stumbled around for a few minutes until he realized she was screaming and crying from the spare bedroom, not his bedroom. She continued to yell as Sam ran to her side and asked her what was wrong. She told him someone had brought her to the bedroom, stripped her bottoms, assaulted her, and raped her. She said, "He was on top of me trying to have sex with me. I woke up, and then he hit me in the face and knocked me out.

Sam said, "Hold on, I'm going to see if he's still in the house." He grabbed a baseball bat and ran through the house, searching every room and bumping into the walls along the way. Not finding the guy, he returned to her side to comfort her. She was sobbing as she put her panties and skirt back on, went back to the couch, and sat down at one end.

She was rocking back and forth in a fetal position and crying. She said, "Who would do something like that? I'm going to find out who did this to me, and I'm going to kill the son of a bitch."

Sam said, "Not if I get to him first. That fucker has to be someone we know, someone we've been having over for our parties. We'll find out who it was, I promise. I can't believe he would be that stupid and bold to think he could get away with doing that to you."

She replied, "Yeah, that took a lot of balls for him to try something like that in your house and while you were in the next room, lying on the couch. Whoever it is, he's plain crazy."

They couldn't sleep for the rest of the night as they smoked some more pot to calm their nerves.

He and Ashley had decided not to tell anyone what happened to Ashley in hopes they could find out who it was without him becoming suspicious.
Sam spent the next few days talking to some girls at his house the night of the party. Sam asked the girls if they noticed anyone acting weird or doing anything different while they were there that night. One of his closest friends told him that Sean Thomas was conducting a little odd that night, and he was the last to leave the house. She said, "I know because we were the last ones to leave, and Sean's car was still there when we left. I figured he had car trouble, or maybe he got so wasted that he crashed into one of your extra bedrooms." Sam thanked her and asked her not to say anything to Sean or anyone else about their conversation.

When Sam told Ashley who it was, she was outraged. She said, "I knew that guy was a snake. I never trust him. You should let me kill that guy myself."

Sam replied, "We have to think about what we want to do without being blamed for his death."

They wanted Sean to think he got away with what he'd done to her. They felt that he would be stupid enough to come to another after-hours party at the house. They devised a plan to get rid of Sean and said they were having a big get-together party again on Friday night.

All the regular friends showed up, and so did Sean Thomas. When he first entered the house, he acted sheepishly and stood off in the back, away from Ashley and Sam. They couldn't believe that he had the guts to show his face after what he had done. They looked at each other, and she raised her eyebrow, smiled a nervous smile, and said, "Man, he's got balls."

They pretended nothing ever happened as they laughed and smoked pot with their friends. After a while, they invited Sean to come and join them and smoke some pot with them. He had been drinking and was a little drunk, so he agreed. It took everything in their power to keep from pulling out a gun and putting a bullet in his head right there. Ashley had told Sam she wanted to rip his eyeballs out of his head once he was dead.

When it was Sean's time to smoke, Sam pulled out a fresh new cigarette and handed it to him. Sean quickly lit it and took a couple of deep inhales of the weed. Sean didn't realize that the cigarette contained some highly potent fentanyl drugs. It only took a few hits before he felt the poison's effects and dropped the cigarette to the floor. Ashley pretended the cigarette had caught something on fire when it fell. She had a small hand towel sitting next to her. She immediately grabbed the cigarette, wrapped it in the towel, ran to the bathroom with the stuff, and flushed it down the toilet. Ashley did not want other friends to pick it up and smoke the deadly poison. She then returned to be by Sam's side.

It wasn't long before Sean started to shake and gasp for air as his body temporarily stiffened. He tried to get up but fell to the floor. As he fell to the floor, Sam and Ashley bent down next to him, and Sam whispered in his ear, "Your dead motherfucker, you fucked up. Maybe you shouldn't have done that to my girl. Did you think you could get away with raping her?" He looked up at Sam and then glanced over at her with his red face and eyes bugged out, but he couldn't say anything as he took his last breath.

They each put his arms under their shoulders, grabbed an arm, and carried him to the spare bedroom. They put him on the same bed where he'd assaulted and raped Ashley. She said, "This is ironic. You get to use that bed, after all, mother fucker. You almost got away with what you did to me, you stupid son of a bitch". She punched Sean's body in the balls with her fist. When they came out of the bedroom, Sam told everyone that Sean had too many drugs and needed to sleep them off. He told everyone to leave him alone so that he could stay the night.

After everyone left in the early morning hours, it was still dark outside. Sam and Ashley took Sean's body and put it in his car. Sam wore gloves as he drove Sean's car to the rough part of town and parked in an empty parking lot. He pulled Sean's body over to the driver's side to make it look like he was the one that had been driving. She followed behind in Sam's vehicle, and once they knew nobody had seen what they did, they went back to Sam's house.

When they got home, sitting on the couch, she said, "That guy had a lot of nerve to try and pull off something like that. I'm glad he's dead. He deserves what he got. He's probably done that shit to other girls before and got away with it."

Sam replied, "Yeah, he was a real winner. I need to be a little more cautious about who I let come to my house and party with us in the future. I'm sorry that happened to you, Ashley. At least we won't have to worry about him ever doing it again to you or anyone."

***

Chapter 14 - Finding out about Kari's Assault

The next day when she got home after being raped, Jackson saw the bruises on her face and asked her what had happened. He said, "Did you and Sam have a fight like you and Seth had that night when you killed him?"

She put her head down and said, "No, it was nothing like that. Maybe I'll tell you about it someday." After what she said to Jackson when the three guys in the Center raped him, she was too embarrassed to tell him what happened to her.

He just shook his head and didn't say anything else but whispered, "When will she ever learn she can't hang out with those loser drug addicts?"

He spent hours playing games on the computer when he decided to venture downtown again. He wanted to see what was going on there. He went to some of his old familiar places. Still, He then decided to go to a new area of town where he'd never been before—the Old

Town Bakersfield section, where they had several excellent restaurants, bars, and other businesses.

As he walked around for a few hours, he ran into a girl who called out his name as he walked by her. It was one of his friends from grade school, Kari Simmons. She always liked her but hadn't seen her in several years. She was a lot different now, more grown-up and outgoing. She had a skateboard in her hands and was wearing the normal knee and elbow pads as she approached him. Her dark hair was in a ponytail under the helmet, and he thought she looked cute. She asked him a few questions and asked if he had time to sit and talk. They grabbed a soft drink and found a place to sit and talk about school and what each of them had been up to since they had last seen each other.

He lied to her and said he hadn't been doing much, just staying home and spending time playing video games on his computer. He told her that his life had been pretty dull and unexciting. He then asked her how things had been with her. She told him a little about high school and her friends, and they talked at length about just stuff in general.

Once Kari felt comfortable with him, she lowered her head and said, "I'm going to tell you about something that happened to me, but it's very private, and I don't like to talk about it with just anyone. I consider us friends so that I can share it with you."

He said, "Whatever it is, your secret is safe with me. I don't tell anybody anything. Not even my mom anymore."

She said, "Right after I last saw you, it was when I was in the sixth grade. I was eleven when a neighbor pulled me into his house and raped me. None of us knew then that he liked having sex with young girls. He seemed like a friendly, nice neighbor guy who always talked with me when he saw me alone. When he moved in next to us, we didn't know that he was a pedophile and had gotten in trouble with young girls.

After he raped me, the police arrested him and imprisoned him, but they only kept him there for a few years. The courts decided they wanted to try and rehabilitate him. The authorities told my parents and me that they believed he wasn't a true pedophile that focused on his sexual attraction to a child but rather an opportunistic pedophile that just took advantage of a situation. Since we lived next door, I was easy prey for the opportunist."

Jackson interrupted her and said, "That is bullshit. They should have hung the sorry SOB."

She laughed and replied, "Right, huh!"

"During the court trial, he tried to minimize what happened to me to the point that he almost didn't believe, in his mind, that he did anything to me. His lawyer claimed he was also sexually molested when he was a child, so somehow, that made it all ok, and they felt like they could cure him of his problem."

He listened intently to her story as he sat there. He felt his face flush with anger as his blood began to boil. The thought of someone doing horrible sexual things to her when she was just a kid overwhelmed him. Because his mom was also a victim of a pedophile, he had a particular dislike for those types of people. He felt like they had no place in society and should be eliminated.

He also confided in her and said, "My mom was kidnapped when she was nine years old and held captive for seven years. She was repeatedly raped for years by a guy named Charlie, that kidnapped her. She has never gotten over the pain of that happening to her."

Kari had tears in her eyes as she said, "I know I will never get over what happened. It will be with me for the rest of my life too. I still have nightmares that he broke into our house and raped me again. I live in fear of him all the time because he is free and living here in Bakersfield. I fear he could show up again at our house anytime."

He replied, "I hope you know and understand it wasn't your fault that he raped you. You didn't do anything wrong. You were just a kid and a victim, just like my mom."

Kari said, "I know that now, but I blamed myself for what he did to me for the first few years after it happened. I felt like I should never have been so friendly with him. I've had to deal with the embarrassment and shame of what happened to me during the trial. I felt like people were always staring at me, and at first, I was afraid to show my face at school."

He said, "I know how you feel. My mom told me she went through the same thing."

He asked her if she knew where the guy lived in Bakersfield.

She replied, "They let him out, and he lives several miles from here, and my mom and dad keep track of him. My dad initially wanted to kill him but didn't want to go to jail for the rest of his life for killing the scumbag."

They continued talking about him, and Jackson casually asked if she knew the guy's name and address.

She said, "Yes, I have it, they have to let people know when a pedophile moves into a neighborhood, so I looked up everything about him when I got older." She told him his name was Stephen Ayers and gave him the address where he was living. She said, "I feel like my father. I'd kill him if I could get away with it, but I don't have the guts. I know he's probably still doing that to other kids. I don't care what the courts say. He should be imprisoned for the rest of his life."

Jackson replied, "Yeah, that or dead."

They talked for about an hour, and Jackson enjoyed talking with her. They promised to meet up again sometime soon as they exchanged phone numbers as said their goodbyes. On the way home, he couldn't get the entire experience she had been through off his mind. Somehow, he kept relating her experience to what his mom's horrible experience must have been like. Thinking about it started to eat at him. The more he thought about what Kari told him, the more he wanted to do something to the guy. He couldn't believe that now the guy was a free man, and she had to live with the torment and pain he had caused her for the rest of her life. He whispered, "Man, this life isn't fair. How can these people keep getting away with things when others spend years in prison for fewer crimes? I'm glad my dad killed the guy that kidnapped my mom."

When he got home, he did a lot of research about pedophiles to see if he could familiarize himself with them. Kari's ordeal sparked his interest, and he wanted to learn everything he could about Pedophiles. He soon learned they usually have a lower IQ and impaired motor skills. They possess shame, low self-esteem, and social avoidance. Still, and most importantly, they are sexually attracted to children, either boys or girls. He also found that most pedophiles are males.

He couldn't believe it when he found that reports said not everyone who sexually molests a child is a pedophile because they may not have an ongoing sexual attraction to children. They take advantage of situations and can't refrain from their sick impulses. He felt that might be the case with Kari, but it didn't make any difference. As far as he was concerned, her molester was in the same category as the others. He strongly desired to find out where the guy lived and kill him.

***

Chapter 15 - Going after the Pedophile

The name and address of the Pedophile, Stephen Ayers, that had attacked Kari was rooted deep in his memory. No matter what Jackson did each day for the next few weeks, he couldn't get the pedophile off his mind. Searching the public records, Jackson found the police report from when Ayers was first arrested and went before the Judge. During his trial, his defense was that a demon-possessed him when he attacked her. He claimed the demon inside of him did those things to Kari and not him. While reading the report, he smiled and shook his head as he thought, "Some people might believe you, Ayers, but I'm not buying your story."

While thinking about Ayers, he had all the visions of what he might look like and how he may act. He soon became obsessed with finding out more about Ayers and even confronting him at his house. He located his address on Bakersfield's map and calculated how long it would take to ride his bike to Ayer's house. He figured it would take almost an hour to get there and another hour to get back home.

He was anxious to check things out but was patient and waited a few weeks before he started going to Ayer's home. He waited until after his mom left for work, and it was dark before he took off in a westerly direction and deeper into the older part of town. When he found Ayer's house, he quickly found a place to hide himself and his bike behind bushes across the street from his home. There was an open area big enough to get himself and his bicycle behind the tall and bushy Oleander bushes. It appeared as though someone had used the place before. Maybe even a homeless person. He had a good view of Ayer's house from behind the bushes without being spotted by someone. There was a light on the outside front porch, and he sat there and watched for a few hours. He wanted to see if Ayers lived alone, had a wife, or if someone else was living there with him.

His house was in an older neighborhood with older homes. He believed most were wooden, small two to three-bedrooms with one bathroom, and built around the 1950s. After going to the house a few times and checking things out, he snuck up and peeked through the window to see what Ayers was doing. When he first looked through the window of his house, he saw Ayers sitting in a recliner and watching television. Waiting a few minutes, Ayer got up and slowly went to the kitchen. He was surprised that he was looking at the face of an older man with graying hair around his temples, who walked slowly and slightly stooped over. He whispered, "I can't believe this guy is the one that did that to Kari. He looks old and battered." After being satisfied that Ayers lived alone, he left and headed home.

A few days later, Jackson returned to Ayer's house again, but it was during the day. He parked his bike in the familiar hiding place and waited until he built up the nerve to go across the street and confront Ayers. He wanted to learn more about the older man who had felt compelled to rape his friend Kari when she was a young girl. He boldly and confidently walked up to the raised and covered front porch and knocked on the door. He knocked on it several times before Ayers came to the door.

Ayers opened the door and saw Jackson standing there. Before he had a chance to say anything, Ayers said gruffly, "What the hell do you want, kid?" Jackson stepped back a few steps, not expecting that type of reaction from him. He lied and said, "I heard you might need someone to do a little work around here. I'm looking for a job and would be glad to help you with whatever you need to have done."

Ayers stared at him for a few seconds with an angry look on his wrinkled face and said, "Who the hell told you that? I don't need anything done, especially from the likes of you."

He said, "I'm sorry if I offended you, sir. I wanted to make extra money to help with my school things."

Ayers replied, "Well, I don't have anything for you, so get the hell off my porch and get out of here." Then he slammed the door in Jackson's face.

Jackson stood on the porch for a few more seconds to collect his thoughts. He thought, "What a pathetic and sorry excuse for an individual. Life hasn't been good to him because he's nothing but a bitter and broken old man." He was angry that Ayers had treated him so rudely. The anger went all over his body, and he defiantly knocked several more times until Ayers opened the door again, and now, he was angry as he said, "What the hell is up with you, kid? I thought I clarified that I don't need your fucking help with anything."

His anger got the best of him as he said sternly, "Do you remember what you did to Kari Simmons, asshole?" You assaulted and raped her when she was only eleven years old. Do you remember doing that, sir?"

Ayers looked him in the eyes and said, "Yes, I remember, but I paid my dues for what they said I did to her, so get out of here before I call the cops and have you arrested."

He believed this guy had convinced himself of his lies, that he never did anything to Kari, it was the demon inside of him, and he didn't deserve to be labeled a Pedophile. Perhaps he thought the looks and the treatment he'd received from people in the neighborhood once they found out he was a Pedophile were unjustified.

He had to restrain himself as he thought, "Man, I was nice to that fucking guy, and he treated me like I was nothing but a punk kid." It made him angry Ayers had treated him that way, but now he knew this was the right person he was after. He also knew he didn't want Ayers to live the rest of his life thinking he got away with doing those disgusting and horrible things to Kari. He wondered how many other girls Ayers had attacked but never got caught.

He knew he had to get out of there, or Ayers probably would've called the cops on him, as he threatened. He immediately turned around and started to walk away. He knew he had to get back home to plan his strategy on what he would do to that piece of crap.

He waited a few weeks until there was no moon out, and it was pitch black in the night. He
put on his dark clothing. He then put the duct tape, a sharp butcher knife, and one loaded pistol in his backpack. He then headed to Ayer's house and got there while he was still up watching television. He parked his bike in its familiar hiding spot across the street. He watched the neighborhood for about thirty minutes to see any street activity.

When he felt comfortable, he pulled the sock cap down over his hair and ears, took the gun from the backpack, and headed across the street. He crept slowly up to the window and peeked inside, and Ayers was sitting in his favorite recliner. He looked around and made sure nobody watched him, then went to the front door and knocked. Ayers reluctantly opened the door after a few hard and persistent knocks.

When he opened the door, Jackson immediately pushed it open with his leg and body as he stuck a gun to Ayer's head and said, "Hey, remember me motherfucker? You should've been nicer to me, old man." Not waiting for an answer, he motioned Ayers back away. He had him sit down on the couch. He quickly went to the curtains and closed them shut so that nobody could see inside

Ayers yelled out, "What the hell do you want from me? I never did anything to you?"

He quickly pulled out the duct tape, put on his gloves, tore a six-inch piece off, and stuck it across Ayer's mouth. He then immediately wrapped Ayer's hands behind his back with tape. Once he had Ayers tied up, he picked him up and led him into the kitchen by his shirt's collar.

Before he sat Ayers down, he unbuckled his belt and pulled down his pants and underwear past his knees. Ayers tried to hit him with his shoulder when he did that, so Jackson instantly hit him across the face with his elbow, knocking him semi-unconscious. He grabbed him before falling to the floor and made him sit in one of the kitchen chairs with a back. He wrapped duct tape around his feet, put a couple of strands around his body and feet, and then around the chair so that Ayers couldn't move.

He carefully took out the sharp butcher knife and said, "What kind of sick pleasure does a guy get out of raping a little girl who is only eleven years old? I wonder how many other young girls you did that too and got away without getting caught?" He didn't want an answer to that question either. He just wanted Ayers to know that was why he would die.

Ayers squirmed around, trying to get free as Jackson reached down with his left hand and grabbed Ayer's penis and testicles in the palm of his left hand. He quickly cut everything off with the knife in his right hand and threw them on the floor. The blade cut through his skin and tissue-like cutting through soft butter. Ayers tried to scream in pain, but the duct tape muffled his voice. He looked down at the blood spurting from his castrated body, and his eyes widened with fear. He knew it was just a matter of time before he would be bleeding to death.

Jackson said, "When you get to hell, you will get your just reward for what you've done here on Earth to these young girls. I hope it was all worth it for you. Now you can finally meet the demon you claimed was inside you that made you do it to the girls."

He was careful not to step in any blood as he went to the sink and washed the blood from his knife before putting it into his bag. He waited until Ayers bled out and wasn't getting a pulse before putting his bag on his back, going over, opening the curtains, and peeking outside. He wanted to make sure nobody was watching the house as he left.

Not seeing anyone, he slowly opened the front door and stepped outside. He locked and closed the door behind him. He stood with his back to the front door for a few seconds to try and get his night vision back. He looked up and down the street in both directions and then crept back to his hiding place across the street. He waited for several minutes until he was comfortable, then got on his bike and quickly left the neighborhood.

It was well past midnight when he got home, and he was exhausted from the ordeal. It didn't take long, and he was fast asleep.

He waited about two weeks and then called Kari. She was happy to hear from him, and they talked for over a half-hour. He was anxious to hear if she had heard about Ayers, but he wasn't going to say anything to her about him.

During their conversation, she said, "Hey, guess what, Jackson? Remember me telling you about the guy that raped me?"

Jackson slowly said, "Yes, I remember."

"Well, they found him dead in his home. Someone went into his house, castrated, and killed him. They cut off his penis and his testicles. Can you believe that? The police came out and questioned my dad thinking he may have been the one that killed him. My dad told the police he didn't do it but was glad the guy was dead because he finally got what he deserved."

Jackson said, "That's great news. You no longer have to worry about that guy coming after you anymore. Maybe you can finally have peace of mind knowing he's not still doing that to girls. You can now release that threat from your memory." They talked a little longer and agreed to call each other again in a few weeks.

***

Chapter 16 - Bully Confrontation

Jackson waited three weeks before he called Kari and asked her if she would like to meet him at the same place for lunch. They hadn't seen each other since the last time they talked. She was happy to hear from him and quickly agreed and asked him to meet her Saturday afternoon around five.

Kari was right on time, but this time didn't have her skateboard and gear with her. Jackson thought she looked pretty in her casual attire and warm coat. Her hair was down, and she appeared more relaxed and happier. When he first saw her, he said, "Wow, you look pretty with your hair down and everything." Kari thanked him, and they made small talk as they began to walk into the restaurant, where they could go inside and eat. Jackson walked his bike to the front door, found a place to attach the chain, and locked it.

They each had a cheeseburger, fries, and a soft drink and talked for about two hours. After a while, Kari smiled and said she needed to return home before her mom and dad started worrying about her. She called her mom about fifteen minutes before she pulled up out front and honked. He followed her out, walked her to the car, and met Kari's mom. He told Kari he would call her in a few weeks and keep in touch. She smiled at him before jumping into the car, happy he would call her again.

After she left, he went back to the restaurant and got his bike. He was heading home when he heard a commotion near the middle of the town square. There was a lot of yelling and girls screaming, and the closer he got to it realized it was a fight. But it wasn't a typical fight. A group of goys was around thirteen to fifteen years old, calling younger boys names and making fun of him. A more prominent and much heavier boy was kicking and punching him in the face while he was down. The younger and smaller boy he picked on seemed scared to death and wasn't standing up for himself. He was lying defenseless on the ground, and the bully seemed to feed off his fear. He could've cared less about the younger boys' feelings as he continued to beat on him.

The bully appeared to know the other boy from school and had decided he wanted the boy's bicycle. He would forcefully take it from him, and nobody was doing anything to stop him.

Jackson was momentarily stunned that a group of children and a few adults gathered around just watching. Everyone seemed amused by the whole thing. Not getting any resistance from the adults, the bully appeared to take extra pride in getting his audience's attention.

Jackson was almost sixteen years old, was five feet ten inches tall, and weighed one hundred and seventy pounds. He had become solid, buffed, and knew how to take care of himself in a fight. The bully's actions toward the weaker boy brought back all those memories of the Juvenile Detention Center.

He didn't have any camouflage with him but was outraged at what he saw. He felt compelled to act. He wasn't going to stand idly by and watch the bully do any more harm to his victim. He yelled out to the adults of the crowd, "What the hell is wrong with you people? Why don't you stop this? Are you all crazy?"

Not getting any response from anyone, he quickly ran up behind the bully and tackled him to the ground. Once he had the kid down, he told him to lie there and not try to get up, or he would hurt him. He yelled out to everyone to go home; the show was over.

The crowd of children and adults began to disperse when he did that. Some of the bully's friends were yelling obscenities at Jackson as they left. When everyone was gone, the bully and his victim were lying on the ground next to each other.

He grabbed the bully by his shirt's collar, stood him up, walked him over to a bench, and sat him down. He then told the younger boy to get his bike and get out of there. He did just as Jackson told him and quickly left.

He said to the bully, "So, how would you like it if I found out where you are every day and decided I was going to beat your ass and take your things from you?"

The bully seemed surprised at the question as he jerked his head up and looked to see how serious he was. Jackson had a mean angry look on his face, and the bully had a few tears in his eyes.

Jackson said, "Do you know how easy it would be for me to do that to you every day for the rest of your life?

I'm one of the guys that hate bullies, and you got lucky this time. Usually, I would follow you on your way home until you were alone somewhere, and then I'd jump and hurt you and put you in the hospital. Maybe break a few bones or two. Do you understand me?" He then told the boy to go home. As he left, he said to the kid, "I'll be watching you. Just remember what I said."

Jackson headed home and tried calming his nerves as he stopped and smoked weed. The confrontation between the boys had brought back some terrible memories. Ones, he was trying hard to forget.

***

Chapter 17 - Breaking into the Drug Dealer's House

Jackson was at the age where he wanted to start driving soon. He took online courses on his computer to get his driver's license and talked to his mom about his wishes. He wanted to start driving a car, and she gave him the money to get him through all the requirements. He became preoccupied with getting his license and didn't go out much. He talked to Kari on the phone as often as she could and felt content during that time.

He received his driver's permit and could drive a car as long as a licensed adult was in the car with him. Ashley began practicing with him on her days off as they went into the country, into the foothills on winding roads, and on the freeway at higher speeds to become efficient and confident in his driving. After a few months, he felt like he was a pro and wanted to drive every time his mom got into the car

When he turned sixteen, he got his driver's license, but there was a problem. He didn't have a car to drive, and the insurance costs for one were too high. It would add a few hundred dollars per month to his mom's auto insurance, and his mom didn't want to pay that much.

She told Jackson, "Since you're not going to school, you need to get a job somewhere so you can get your car and pay your insurance."

He looked at her with apprehension and said, "Mom, who is going to hire a sixteen-year-old? The only job I can get would be at a fast-food restaurant, and they don't pay enough for a car payment, insurance, and the gas I would need."

She replied, "You're a smart kid. I'm sure you will figure it out. Aren't you the one that told me you could take care of yourself and didn't need my help?"

The following day after they talked, he checked around the different fast-food places. After putting in his application to several businesses, he landed a job at one of them. He began working there, and they had him on a schedule of six hours per day, four days a week. After taking out all his deduction from his weekly paycheck, he wouldn't have enough money for a car payment and insurance. He thought, "If something happened to my mom or I wanted to live on my own, I could never afford to get a car or a place on my income." Just thinking about it was a little too hard to comprehend.

He had become impatient because he wanted a car to go wherever he wanted. Jackson thought he and Kari could sometimes go out on a date if he had a car. That would be another expense where he would have to spend money.

He believed he had become vigilant and good at breaking into houses. He figured that would be the easiest and quickest way to get the money needed for his plans. He began researching the area of Bakersfield, where the homes were that were over one million dollars. Once he found his location, he would break into some of those homes on his days off work. While inside, he would look for high-end jewelry that was easy to sell and cash stashed away in little hiding places that were easy to steal. After searching and asking around on the streets to some of his old friends, he was able to find a guy who would purchase the jewelry from him and sell it in Los Angeles.

After several weeks of breaking into some high-end homes, he wasn't making as much headway as fast as he wanted. After watching a large house for several hours, one night, he decided to break into the place within the next few days.

He had seen a lot of activity during the day, but it became quiet at night. He believed it was a drug dealer's home but didn't know it was Juan Carlos Trevino's. He was an illegal drug dealer in Bakersfield who sold many drugs to the people on the streets that Jackson knew.

Someone had parked a few cars in the big circle driveway, but he didn't see anyone moving inside the house. Figuring he might be able to get into the house while the owner was sleeping. He could take a few thousand dollars without it looking as though any money was missing.

He waited until it was a night with no moon and put on all his dark clothing. He strapped on his backpack with his weapons inside and went to the house. He waited in a hiding place where he had earlier watched the house from bushes across the street. He remained hidden until after midnight, all the lights in the house were off, and people were asleep. An outdoor front light lit up the house's entire front, the circle drive, and the yard. It had a small night light left on in the hallway, but no activity was happening there. He crept to the side of the house, where the front light wasn't shining so bright. His hands and knees were slightly shaking as he checked the doors. To his surprise, someone had left the door on the south side unlocked. He slowly opened it very quietly and stepped inside, making sure not to make any sound. He carried a small flashlight in his hand as he carefully crept his way through the dark interior of the large house. He was cautious as he took one step at a time and made his way around.

He knew this was the right place for him because there wasn't much furniture or pictures on the walls. It looked like a place a single guy would live, not a family. He didn't see anything visible he could steal after quickly shining his light on the living room and kitchen table area. He took short, quiet breaths and went to the first bedroom door down the hallway. He slowly opened it and took a glance inside. Not seeing anyone, he shined his light around and was stunned to find that the owner had taken out one of the walls to a connecting bedroom and made the area into a vast receiving and drug distribution area for his drug dealing business. Seeing that he was alone in the room quickly shut the door behind him.

Once he was standing in the room, his heart was pounding loud and fast because now he knew the owner wasn't just an ordinary drug dealer. He knew this guy was a pretty good-sized dealer. Drugs were sitting on a couple of card tables, and money was next to them. Jackson smiled as he thought this was what he was looking to find. He thought he might take a small handful of the money from the table until, flashing his light under one of the tables saw a bag full of cash on the floor. He looked inside the large bag; the money was in six-inch stacks with rubber bands around them. There were a lot of them. Jackson whispered, "Oh, man, this is the mother lode."

Jackson instinctively grabbed six of the stacks of money without thinking about any repercussions or consequences and put them in his bag on his back. Once he had the money inside, he immediately opened the door and stepped into the hallway. Not seeing or hearing anyone stirring in the house, Jackson quietly began to make his way to the back door, where he came into the house. Just as he opened the door to leave, He listened to the loud barks of a giant dog. It sounded like a Rottweiler or one of that size, and the sound was coming from the back master bedroom. It sent fear through his body as he whispered, "Fuck me, I have to get out of here now."

Just as he stepped outside, he heard the dog coming down the hallway after him. He quickly closed the door and started running for his bicycle. Just as he got on it and started to pedal away, he heard growling and barking from the dog. The people inside the house had let him out, and he now was charging at Jackson at full speed. He knew there was no way to outrun the dog, so he went about two hundred yards, then jumped off his bike and pulled the metal weapon out of this backpack. Jackson was breathing hard as he wrapped the string handle around his wrist and gripped it tightly. He readied himself for the charging dog as he took a fighting stance. Jackson quickly stepped to one side and hit the dog hard across the head just as it plunged at him. It let out a yelp as he hit it a second time, and it fell to the ground. It seemed dazed and scared as it got up, put its bobbed-off tail between its legs, and started slowly trotting back toward the house. He quickly got back on his bike with his weapon still in his hand and started peddling as fast as possible to get out of the subdivision.

When the dog came out of the house, all the lights came on inside the home. The place lighted up like a Christmas tree. He could see a lot of activity going on as he looked back over his shoulder as he rode away. Several men with automatic weapons came out of the house, watching the dog as it chased and then returned. One of the men yelled out that he got a glimpse of someone on a bicycle, and he ran into the house and got his keys to his car. He was almost three-quarters of a mile away when two men got in their vehicle and came after him. The man had a huge spotlight and shone it in the tall bushes along his path. Jackson was far enough away that he was able to take another exit road and escape unseen.

His breathing was heavy because of the extra adrenaline. Once he felt safe, he slowed his breathing and took a couple of deep breaths. His heart was still beating fast as he released a massive sigh of relief from getting away from the men. He believed the men were sleeping in a couple of the other bedrooms. He shivered when he thought about what they would have done to him if he had gone into one of those rooms and they had caught him. He knew they wouldn't waste any time killing him.

He didn't know why the owner had his dog in the room with him instead of roaming the rest of the house, but he felt lucky it wasn't. If it would've caught him inside, it may have ripped him to shreds before he could get his weapon out. He whispered, "I love dogs, but I don't want to get killed by one."

When he got home, he hid the bag of money in his secret hiding place and, after smoking some weed to calm himself down, went to bed for the night.

The following day when he got up, retrieved the bag, and counted the money, there were six hundred thousand dollars in total in the six stacks. He took a slow breath when he finished counting it and said, "Holy fuck, I'm in real trouble now. If that drug dealer finds out I was the one that took his money, he'll come after me and kill me. I can't even take the money back now because he'd still kill me for stealing it from him in the first place."

When Carlos learned from his first in command, Miguel Estrada, he raced about the missing money. He asked Miguel how the person had gotten into the house and stolen the money without anyone hearing or seeing him. He wondered if there were any broken windows or doors. Miguel checked all the windows and doors and discovered the door the men used had been unlocked.

Miguel told him that one of the men saw someone riding a bicycle, but he was too far away to see much in the dark.

Carlos said, "Find out who was the last person to use that door and not lock it and kill him. Then take his body out to the country and dispose of him."

Miguel replied, "I'll take care of that, Boss."

Carlos was angry and shouting aloud as he went about the house. He screamed, "The one night I have my dog in my bedroom, and this happens." The rest of the men were standing around, not knowing what to say or do next. Carlos continued to shout, "Does the guy think he can get away with stealing my cash? We need to find out who did this and kill him."

Miguel replied, "We'll find out who it was and take care of him."

***

Chapter 18 - Carlos sends his Thugs

Jackson spent the next several days at home contemplating what to do with the money. He soon felt the money was of no use to him since he couldn't spend it anywhere. He realized things for him would have been better off leaving Calos' money alone and walking away.

When it came to the money, he was screwed. He couldn't spend large amounts of it at one time without it getting around on the streets and back to Carlos. Once he found out, he would send his men after Jackson. They would want to know how that much money ended up in his hands, and he wouldn't have a simple answer for them. He could lie and say he broke into many houses and sold items, and that's how he got the money. He couldn't put that much cash in the bank all at once because the Feds would ask him how that much money came into his possession. He couldn't laundry the money on the streets because Carlos' men would find out. He couldn't give it to anyone or tell anyone about it, or they may slip and tell the wrong person it was him.

He decided to leave the money hidden for now and go back to his everyday life of breaking into expensive houses and stealing things at night while working at the restaurant during the day. He believed that was his only way of keeping the people in the streets from becoming suspicious of him and telling Carlos. Though some of the roads were his friends, they had no loyalty to anyone except themselves. He had to return to what he was doing before stealing the money.

About a week later, he brought his contact on the street some expensive jewelry he'd stolen and asked him to sell it for him. Jackson was back in business. But now, he was a little more cautious and a lot more paranoid while dealing with people in the streets. He was always watching his back to make sure nobody was following him. Jackson began to circle back a few times on his bike home to make sure he was alone. He realized Carlos and his men were killers and would do anything to get his money back. They wouldn't think twice about killing him and his loved ones and dumping their bodies somewhere in the desert. He did it with his men. He knew he didn't only have to protect himself but also his mom. He believed the best way to do that was to pretend the money didn't exist.

Once things went back to normal, he began to call Kari, and they would meet a few times a week to have lunch or dinner. Their relationship was starting to blossom into more than just friends. They liked each other very much. During that time, Kari asked Jackson if he would ever buy a car to go out on an actual date with each other. He didn't tell her he had the cash to purchase any car he wanted but was afraid to use the money. He said, "Sure, I'll buy a car one of these days. I have to make enough money first."

The more they would meet, the more the pressure for him to buy a car became. He always told Kari that he was saving money to buy one but wasn't ready yet.

During one of their luncheons, she asked Jackson, "Aren't you tired of riding that bicycle all over the place? You're going to be seventeen soon. Are you going to ride it forever?"

When she said that to him, he temporarily took offense to what she said because he liked riding his bike. He replied, "Yeah, I'm going to get a car soon. I'm still waiting for the right moment and the right car." He didn't tell her he was just a little afraid to buy a car. He didn't want the word to get back to Carlos that a young guy that rode a bike all over town paid a lot of cash to buy a car.

A few weeks later, caving into Kari's pressure, he took some cash out of its hiding place and went to a local car dealership. He paid money for a 2015 used silver dodge charger with a black interior. He also paid for his insurance one year in advance with cash. It had been several months since he first stole the money, and Jackson hoped Carlos had moved on from someone taking his money.

Kari was happy he bought the car, but Jackson believed he would be in trouble if the street guys found out. He decided to continue using his bicycle when breaking into houses and on the streets. He would keep the Charger parked in the garage and only use it on special occasions.

When Ashley asked Jackson where the money came from to purchase the vehicle was, he told her he'd saved his money. She rolled her eyes because she knew he was still breaking into houses. She said, "Don't get caught again."

Then Jackson's fears began to come true. A few weeks later, when Jackson talked to some of his street friends, he noticed a man watching him. He kept a close eye on the guy and saw that he was shadowing his every move. Every place Jackson went, the guy followed not too far behind him. Jackson knew it was probably one of Carlos' men. He whispered, "Oh crap, they're on to me now."

Jackson had his weapon and a pistol in his backpack and decided he'd find out what this guy wanted with him. He ensured the guy was behind him as he turned into a dark alley away from all the main street action. He watched as the guy followed him into the dark alley. There were no lights on in the place, and it was pitch black. He went about forty yards into the alley and hid behind some lumber stacked against the wall.

Jackson jumped out from behind with his weapon and struck him across the head as the guy approached him. Once the guy was on the ground, Jackson had his gun out and put it to his head.

He asked the guy, "Why are you following me." At first, he wouldn't say anything, so Jackson asked him again. "You better tell me, or I'll kill you right here. Do you understand me?"

Seeing that Jackson wasn't fooling around, the guy reluctantly said, "I work for a guy named Carlos. Do you know him?"

Playing dumb, Jackson said, "No, I don't know him. What does he have to do with me?"

The guy said, "He thinks you might be the one that stole his money."

Jackson quickly asked, "What money?"

The guy wouldn't tell him what money was but said, "Someone came into his house and stole a bunch of cash from him. He's trying to find out who it is and thought it might be you."

Jackson asked, "What makes Carlos think it might be me?"

The guy said, "Because you ride a bike all over town, and you break into houses. That's all I know. I have orders to follow you to see if you were spending much money on the streets. He wanted to know if I could find out if you were the right guy."

Jackson replied, "You go back and tell Carlos I don't know anything about him or his money. The next time he sends a guy after me, I will kill him. Now get the fuck out of here."

He let the guy go, hoping he would tell Carlos that he wasn't the guy who had taken the money. Jackson whispered, "Fuck me. Carlos knows I'm the guy. It's just before they will come after me and kill me."

Jackson began to wonder why Carlos thought he was the guy that took his cash. "Maybe it was because he rode around the streets all the time on his bicycle? Maybe someone on the streets told his men to keep an eye on me? Maybe they somehow found out I paid cash for my car?" He wondered how they could find out about that, but people like Carlos had connections. Whatever made Carlos suspicious of him, he knew they thought it might be him. Then it hit him like a ton of bricks. They saw him leave Carlos' house on the bike the night he broke into it.

He then became paranoid, trying to figure out what to do to protect himself. Jackson knew he would have to become more vigilant in keeping his eyes open if they came after him again.

The man Jackson attacked in the alley returned to Miguel and told him what had happened. He said Jackson told him he didn't know Carlos or anything about money. Miguel said, "No, he's our guy. He has to be the one. How many kids his age has the guts to put a gun to a man's head and threaten to kill him just for following him? Does he also have a reputation for breaking into houses and stealing things? We have to find this kid again, and the next time we'll bring him back here. We'll force him to tell us where the money is hidden. The next time I'll send someone with you to get him."

Jackson decided he would lay low for a while. Maybe Carlos' men wouldn't be able to find out anything more about him if they couldn't find where he lived. He spent the next month calling and hanging out with Kari and tried to pretend the entire Carlos thing would go away.

Not wanting to spend any of Carlos's money, he got low on cash and needed to break into some houses. He had to have things to sell to the guy in the streets. He knew that spending time on the streets because of his connections to sell his items may be a distraction. He was hoping that would throw Carlos' men off his trail. It would show that he was still needing money and not spending the cash.

Jackson had only been in the streets a few days when he spotted the same Mexican guy he had confronted in the alley following him again. Jackson pretended he didn't see the guy but looked around and noticed another guy who seemed interested in his every move. At first, he wasn't sure what to do but wondered if the guy was stupid enough to follow him into the alley again.

Jackson fooled around for a while, talking to some of his friends. Then began to stroll toward one of the alleys off the main street. He was about fifty yards ahead of them when he walked into the alley. He quickly found a place to hide. As they entered the alley, the two men had their weapons drawn, thinking Jackson was also armed.

Jackson didn't waste any time as he killed one of the men. It just happened to be the one he had confronted the last time. The guy with him quickly began to fire his gun in Jackson's direction. It was so dark in the alley that he was shooting wildly, and the bullets bounced off the concrete walls. Jackson returned the gunfire with several rounds.

Jackson could get back out of the alley during the ensuing gun battle without being hit by any bullets. He got back on his bicycle and rode as fast as he could toward his house. Once on his way home, he thought, "Why did that idiot come back in the alley after me? He should've known I would kill him. Now he's dead for that foolish mistake." He knew the guy that got away would go back and tell Carlos what happened. He knew they would be after him with a vengeance now.

Later that day, Miguel found out about his dead friend and immediately went to Carlos and let him know that the kid had killed one of his men. When Carlos heard about it, he yelled, "What the fuck! Are you kidding me? You mean, that kid did that to one of my men?" Carlos went up to Miguel, got in his face, and softly asked, "Do you believe a sixteen-year-old kid stole my money and killed one of my men?"

Miguel replied, "Yes, Boss, I'm sure of it now. This kid is more than what he appears. I think he's a cold-blooded killer, and we must be a little more cautious with him."

Carlos said, "Take a couple of your top men, find out where he lives, force him to tell you where my money is, and then kill him. Kill everyone in his house that lives with him."

Miguel replied, "I will find out for sure and let you know after I have your money and he's dead."

Jackson was in turmoil and knew that his mom had to know about everything he'd done. He didn't want her to be a victim of his reckless actions. The day after Jackson killed the man. He told Ashley they needed to talk about something important. She could tell it was something serious because he seemed nervous as he paced up and down the living room floor.

She looked up from the couch and said, "Ok, Jackson, just tell me what you have done now."

He replied, "I screwed up, broke into the house of a drug dealer in Bakersfield, and took some cash from his home."

She immediately asked how much cash. He replied, "I took six stacks of money, put them into my backpack, and left. When I got home and counted it the next day, I found out it was $600,000.00."

Ashley gasped and said, "Oh, my God, Jackson, that's a lot of money. You're right. You are in big trouble now."

He replied, "I know, the dealer sent a couple of guys after me, and I discovered them following me around. I had them follow me into a dark alley in town, and I killed one of them."

She seemed to be in a state of shock as she said, "Oh, damn. You did what?"

He said again, "I killed one of them. I didn't have a choice. They were going to kill me."

He started telling her about what happened when he took the money. He said, "When I first went into the home, I knew it was a drug dealer's place of business because I had been watching it for a few days. I only wanted to take a few thousand dollars, but I saw the bag full of money, and the temptation was too great. I grabbed the stacks of money without thinking about the consequences and put them in my backpack.

The next day when I realized what a mistake it was, I thought about returning the money. But I figured the drug dealer would still kill me for taking his money in the first place. I've been hiding the cash. I felt like I had to use some money to buy the car and pay for my insurance. The drug dealer somehow found out or suspected me, and that was why his men followed me."

She asked, "So what do you think is going to happen now?"

He said, "I think the drug dealers' men will not give up on me until they get the money back, and I'm dead. Especially after I killed one of their men, I think they will find out my name and where I live and send some of their thugs here to kill me. I'm afraid they may even try to kill you as well. That is why I need to tell you what is happening. Please don't get killed because of me. Maybe you should stay with Sam until all of this blows over, or I'm dead."

She sternly said, "I'm not going to let them run me out of my home. I will defend you and myself if they come and try to kill us. I won't let them kill you."

He said, "Mom, I don't want you to die for my mistake. I wished you would stay with Sam until these things die down."

Then she surprised him and said, "Look, you have yourself in a little bit of a pickle here, but you need to think about how to turn this around. Those men will never quit until you and I are dead. What do you think your dad would do if confronted with this situation? I know he wouldn't sit back and wait for them to come after him. If you know where the drug dealer lives, you may want to consider going after those guys before they can find you and kill you. I'm here for you and will help you any way I can."

He didn't say anything for a few minutes, trying to wrap his head around what she had just said. He couldn't believe she was willing to help him out and kill the guys.

He thought, "Is it possible I could do something like that? Can I truly go after them and try to kill them first?" A shiver went up his spine as he thought about the mere idea.

He thanked his mom for her support and told her he loved her and would figure it out soon. He contemplated how he could go after Carlos and his men and make what she said to happen.

***

Chapter 19 - Killing Carlos' men

The following day Ashley came into Jackson's bedroom and told him she wanted to talk more about what he had told her. She said, "Ok, Jackson, you have these guys that want to kill you, but I'm not going to let that happen. We can make plans to protect you and me without leaving my home. They talked extensively about her different ideas, and he thought some of them might work.

After listening intently, he looked at his mom and said, "Are you sure about this? Do you want to get that involved in this thing? Is that what you want to do? You don't have to do this, and you know I'd rather you didn't."

Ashley replied, "I told you last night I'm not going to sit idly by and let some thugs kill you or me. I will do whatever I must to protect us, even if I have to kill some of them myself. I'm not opposed to doing that."

Jackson said, "Ok, mom, but I don't want anything to happen to you. You are all I have in this world, and I don't know what I'd do if you got killed because of me."

Ashley went over to Jackson, put her arm around him, and said, "You're my whole world, and I love you very much. That is why we're going to do this together. For now, I need you to find a couple of pistols with silencers and two rifles with scopes and silencers. Make sure we have plenty of ammunition for all of them. Take some of that drug money, get what we need, and worry about its costs. Go to town and get a silent alarm for our doors and windows. It will alert us while sleeping in our bedrooms if someone breaks in at night. Get plenty of duct tape and a thin plastic about ten feet by twelve feet in length and width."

Jackson told his mom he would contact a friend and find out where he could go in Los Angeles the following day and get what they needed. That afternoon, he went to the store and got all the wiring and things they needed for the silent alarms. Once he got home, he installed everything and checked them to ensure they worked.

He and Ashley stayed extra vigilant for the next several nights to ensure someone wasn't trying to break into the house. Jackson took two of the guns with silencers he'd gotten in Los Angeles, gave one to Ashley, and said, "Here, you take this one. Are you sure you know how to use this thing?

Ashley replied, "Yes, your dad took me with him a few times and showed me how to shoot a pistol and a rifle. If one of those thugs comes through our door, he'll be a dead man."

Jackson couldn't believe how brave and calloused his mom was about possibly killing the guys. He raised his eyebrows and whispered, "Man, who is this woman? I don't even know her."

Ashley never told Jackson she took credit for killing old Charlie after Cooper killed him at the Cabin. She always secretly wished she were the one that had killed him instead of Cooper. Ashley was chained to that wall the entire time. She thought about different ways to kill Charlie if she ever got free and had the chance. The bitter anger of her captivity was still deep inside Ashley's soul. Even though there was a certain amount of fear, she was excited and determined to help Jackson.

Once the alarms were in place and they had the weapons they needed, they followed Ashley's plan. The two of them left together and headed for the area where he'd killed the guy several days earlier. Ashely wore jeans, a dark-colored sweatshirt with a hoodie, and a pistol tucked underneath.

When they got to the area, they split up, and Ashley went her separate way, but not too far from Jackson. She watched his every move while pretending to be interested in what was going on in the street. They each had their cell phones on so they could keep in touch.

Jackson did what he always did and hung out with a few regulars from the area. He kept looking for the guy with the man he killed or anyone else who seemed to be interested in him. They were there for several hours, but nothing suspicious happened, and the guy didn't show.

They kept a safe distance from each other on the way back. They talked to each other on the cell phone as they made their way home. They didn't know that two of Carlos' men already knew where he lived and had the place staked out.

That night it was around three in the morning when the silent alarms in Jackson and Ashley's room sounded like an intruder. They both knew their plan if this happened and had their weapons ready as they moved over close to their bedroom door. They could hear the shuffling of feet, but it was faint, and Jackson thought, "These guys are good. You would never know they were in the house."

It didn't take long, and one of the intruders slowly made his way to Ashley's bedroom. Ashley whispered, "I hope Jackson is ok. I don't want him to get killed." The guy had his gun out as he slowly opened the door. He had a small flashlight in his left hand. He began to shine the light toward the bed. He was so quiet she could hardly tell he was right in front of her. He was so close she could hear him breathing, and he was standing right next to her. As he shined the light, Ashley put her pistol to his head and instantly pulled the trigger. The gun made a low puff sound, and the fire from the bullet made a little red light. The guy made a thud as he instantly fell dead to the floor.

The other guy with him had chosen Jackson's room, and Jackson was also waiting for him. Just as the other guy opened Ashley's bedroom door, the guy slowly opened Jackson's door simultaneously. He, too, had a small flashlight in one hand and a gun in the other as he followed into the bedroom. As soon as he did that, he heard Ashley's gun and his comrade's body hitting the floor. He instantly knew it was a gunshot with a silencer. He started to turn and check out what had happened, but Jackson shot him in the back of the head just below the left ear as soon as he turned. He was dead on the floor, half in and half out of Jackson's room.

Jackson then crept into the living room to make sure no more intruders were in the house. Not finding any, he called out to his mom to see if she was ok. She immediately told him she was and asked if the other guy he shot was dead. He told her he was, and they both relaxed and met in the living room. Jackson checked to see how they got into the house, and they had picked the locks and cut the chain with bolt cutters. Jackson told his mom they were lucky they had purchased the silent alarms as she had suggested.

Jackson went through their pockets and found the keys to their car. He told his mom to kill anyone that came through the door that didn't identify himself as he went outside and checked around to see if the two guys had any comrades with them. He didn't see anyone else as he walked up and down the street until he found their car parked about two hundred yards away. His heart was beating fast, and he breathed heavily when he returned to the house. The entire time he was gone, Ashley stood by the front door with her pistol pointed upward if someone came through the door. All kinds of things were going through her head as her hands and knees shook. Jackson told her it was him as he returned to the house.

He went over and looked at the bodies. He told his mom that the guy lying on the floor in his bedroom was with the guy he had killed earlier in the alley.

They had previously cut the plastic into two pieces and cleaned them of fingerprints on each side. They put on gloves and rolled each man in a sheet of plastic. Jackson went to the guy's car, backed it up to their garage, and opened the trunk. He left the lights turned off as he backed in so nobody could see what was happening at that time of the morning. They laid an old blanket in the car's trunk, carried the two bodies to the car, and put them on top of the blanket. Jackson placed a gasoline can in the vehicle's trunk with the bodies.

Ashley had already checked out an area where she planned to take the bodies if they killed anyone. It was a location through the small town of Taft and into the foothills. She had also picked out a place where it was dark, secluded, and easy to dispose of the car and bodies. Jackson drove the men's car while she followed close behind in hers. Once she picked out the spot, she flashed the lights to let Jackson know. He immediately pulled over to the side, got out, and poured gasoline on the bodies. He put the car in drive and threw a match on the gas before going over the cliff.

He grabbed the gas can and put it in Ashley's car trunk, and she quickly drove off. They talked about how lucky they were that they hadn't gotten killed by the two guys on the way back home.

Once home, they smoked some pot together to try and relax as they talked some more. Ashley was excited about what had happened and felt good about what they had done together. She said, "We must act fast and go to Carlos's house and kill him and his men before he sends ten guys after us the next time."

Jackson replied, "Yeah, you're right, he will be outraged when his two guys don't return and he finds out they're dead. We should do it within the next few days. For now, let's get some sleep and talk again tomorrow."

That night, as Jackson lay in bed, he thought, "I'm sure glad I have my mom back."

***

Chapter 20 - Going after Carlos and his Men

Jackson knew if he sat around and waited for Carlos's men to come after him, he and his mom would die within a few weeks. His mom was right. They had to go after Carlos and his men before they came after him first. He wasn't sure how many men Carlos still had left because he and his mom had killed three of them already. The following day he sat down with Ashley, and they worked out a plan.

She said, "We must figure out at least four more men left, not counting Carlos."

He replied, "You're right. There have to be at least that many, but probably more. After I broke into the house, I saw at least six or eight guys.

They got all their gear together and planned their attack for the following evening.

It was early evening, and it had just gotten dark as Jackson and Ashley made their way down the dark street where Carlos lived. They had parked several blocks away and made the rest of their way on foot. Each had high-powered rifles with scopes and silencers strapped over their shoulders and pistols in their belt.

They stayed hidden behind the bushes lining both sides of the street as they made their way closer to the house. Jackson was on one side of the road, and Ashley was on the other. When cars came down the street, they ducked behind the bushes.

As they inched their way within fifty yards of the driveway, they found a spot where they could take up a good firing position. The outdoor light lit up the entire front yard, giving Jackson and Ashley enough light to use their scopes. As they watched, two men leisurely walked around the house, and two sat on a couch watching television.

Ashley texted Jackson to let him know she was ready when he was. Jackson told her they would wait until they had a clear shot at two of the men. Once they shot them, they would instantly aim for the other two men. He told her they would count to ten as soon as they ended their texts, then fire on them."

It was silent, except for the crickets chirping and the leaves blowing gently in the breeze. They carefully aimed the rifle at their target, and when they fired, the guns made a puff sound. The bullet casing lit up for a split second, and a puff of smoke entered the night sky. You could hear the glass break as the bullets went through the windows and hit their intended victims. The two men sitting on the couch then jumped up and looked around. They were frantic and shocked at what had just happened to their comrades. They started scurrying around to get their automatic weapons as they tried to find a place to hide. Jackson and Ashley took careful aim, and each took another shot. Jackson's bullet hit his target in the chest, and he also went down. The other one that Ashley shot at ducked just before she fired her shot, and he wasn't hit. He quickly ran to the house's back bedroom. He was yelling at Carlos that they were under attack.

Carlos came running out of his room, saw the damage to his men, and retreated to his bedroom. He first thought he had been raided by the drug enforcement agency or another law enforcement group. But when they didn't storm the house, he knew it wasn't either of those two groups. He figured they wouldn't have stopped by just killing his three men. They would've come on in and gotten them all. As he hid in his bedroom, he wondered what was happening.

Once they went to the back bedrooms, it became a waiting game. Jackson and Ashley knew they couldn't wait there long, or they may end up getting caught or killed themselves. They were in a vulnerable position with just one way out of the subdivision. Jackson knew they would have to let Carlos go for now if they couldn't draw him out of his hiding. They would have to try another time to get him. Carlos and the other man stayed hidden, so Jackson texted his mom after several minutes and told her they had to leave. She agreed, and they took everything and left. They could return to where they had left their car and then head home.

On the way back, Ashley said, "What are we going to do? He'll figure out it wasn't law enforcement that attacked him and probably figured out that you did that to them."

Jackson replied, "Maybe, but we've killed six of his men, so he can't have many left. I know he's got at least one because he ran to the bedroom when we killed his friends. We'll have to figure something out, but now it won't be easy. He will be apprehensive about going anywhere."

Jackson told his mom he was proud of how well she did during the attack. She kept a cool head and was right on in the shooting ability of the men. Ashley felt proud to be doing her part to save her son and herself. She smiled and said, "Thank you, Jackson. I feel better about trying to help you. It's better than waiting for them to come after us."

Carlos and Miguel each survived the attack of Jackson and Ashley, and Carlos was outraged. Now he had three bodies lying on his living room floor, and he had to figure out what to do with them. He couldn't turn over the bodies of the dead men to the authorities because law enforcement would come and investigate everything. They would find out about his drug dealings and throw him in jail. Carlos knew what would happen if the police got involved in any way.

As they surveyed the damage, he told Miguel. "Let's load up these bodies, and you take them out by Mojave and dump them in the desert. They are all illegals, so nobody will know their identity and that they worked for me."

Miguel was still shaken from the attack and said, "What are we going to do, boss, if this kid comes back again? I'm worried he may come back and finish the job and kill both of us."

Carlos replied, "We have to hire a few more men and go after that fucking kid. I know now it was him. Who else would be that bold and stupid? He must know I'd have my men hunt him down and kill him.

Miguel said, "Maybe that was why he did this to us. We sent three of our best men after him, and he killed them. He has killed six men in the last few months since we started going after him. I think he's a lot smarter than we think. Maybe we should leave him alone and forget about the money."

Carlos yelled out, "Are you crazy? I'm not going to let him steal money from me and kill my men and then forget about everything. We'll hunt and kill him, even if I do it myself. Don't we know where he lives?"

Miguel said, "Yes, we do, but it won't do you much good, Boss, if he ends up killing you and me in this process. How do we protect ourselves if he comes after us again? We can't kill someone we can see. We can't stay hidden in this house forever, so what if he comes back to finish the job?"

Miguel feared for his life and thought leaving Jackson alone was the best thing he could do. Because of his fear, he also had doubts about staying and working with Carlos. He didn't think staying with him was worth dying to protect him.

Miguel pulled his car close to the garage as he and Carlos loaded the bodies in the trunk. Miguel told Carlos he had to go to the bathroom and instead detoured into the drug room. He took a stack of cash and put it under his shirt before he left.

He headed over the mountain toward the Mojave Desert. He went deep into the desert, waited until dark, and then dumped the bodies in a secluded place. Once he was finished with that job, it was the last one he would ever do for Carlos. He whispered, "Good luck, boss, I hope he doesn't kill you, but I'm not sticking around to get myself killed along with you." He then headed south toward Los Angeles to make a fresh start. He figured the stack of money was his reward for all the work he'd put in being Carlos's second in command. Now he was done with Carlos and wasn't going back to Bakersfield.

It took Carlos a few days to figure out Miguel wasn't coming back. He didn't know if Jackson had also killed him or what had happened to him, but now he was all alone.

Carlos called in his housekeeper the next day and cleaned up all the dried blood and broken glass. Then he had a window company come out and put in new windows. He had all of them replaced with expensive bullet-proof glass, not wanting to have the same thing happen again.

Jackson and Ashley set silent alarms every night for the next few weeks just in case Carlos sent more men after them.

When they didn't get any activity during those two weeks, Ashley sat Jackson down and said, "I have an idea. Let us see if there is a way to get Carlos's phone number."

Jackson interrupted her and said, "I'm pretty sure I can pull it up on my computer. I can try it, but I'll get it one way or another."

Ashley said, "Once I have his number, I will call him, give him a fake name, and say that I work for a cardiologist here in town. I will tell him that he has an appointment to get a cardiology check-up on a certain day and at a certain time. If he takes the bate and goes on the appointment, you can do a drive-by shooting once he arrives. Or you can walk up to his vehicle and put a bullet in his head at point-blank range. Whichever will work best for you. The police will think it is all gang or drug-related after they go through his home and find all the drugs and money."

Jackson said, "That's a brilliant idea. Let's see if we can get him to fall for the plan. I will find a cardiologist with a parking area that will work for me."

Over the next few days, Jackson checked and found the perfect doctor and location. He also found Carlos's phone number and gave all the information to his mom.

Jackson was sitting next to her as she called Carlos. When he answered, she said, "Hello, is this Juan Carlos Trevino?

He replied, "Yes, this is him."

Ashley continued, "This is Jessica from Doctor Florio's office, and we have you down for a cardiology exam on Thursday morning at 10:00. Will that time be ok with you?

Carlos said, "I didn't set up an appointment with you or anyone else."

Ashley said, "No, your doctor called us and said it was time you had a good cardiology exam because you haven't had one. Will the time and date be good for you?"

Carlos said, "What time and date is that again?" She gave it to him again, and then he asked her for the address.

Ashley gave him the address and said, "So, we'll see you on Thursday at ten in the morning? Try to get here about fifteen minutes early to fill out the paperwork for the doctor." Carlos reluctantly said, "Yeah, I guess I better go." Ashley said, "I'll call you Wednesday afternoon to remind you."

Carlos replied, "Yeah, Yeah, ok, whatever."

Once Ashley confirmed everything, Jackson high-fived his mom and said, "That was great. Now we have to make sure he comes to the appointment." Jackson got everything ready and formulated a plan on how he wanted to kill Carlos.

Just as she said she would do, Ashley called Carlos on Wednesday and reminded him of his appointment the next day. At first, he was trying to make excuses for not wanting to go. Ashley said, "You should make this appointment Mr. Trevino. It takes several months to get a new appointment with Dr. Florio. The only reason he's going to see you is your doctor set it up for you."

Carlos said, "How long will it take?"

Ashley replied, "Only about an hour, then you'll be all done."

Carlos reluctantly said, "Oh, okay, I'll be there."

On Thursday morning, Jackson drove his mom's car to the street where Carlos lived. He didn't know what Carlos looked like and didn't want to kill the wrong person in the parking lot. He waited for Carlos to come driving out of his driveway. Once Carlos started in Jackson's direction, he started his car and went by Carlos, taking a good look at him. He also noticed he had a companion with him. Then he said, "Oh no, he's got his damn dog with him." The huge Rottweiler was sitting on the passenger side with its head raised and looking out the window. From a distance, he almost looked like a person sitting there. He went past Carlos a block, turned around, and turned off on a different street. He sped up and took a shortcut to the medical building. Jackson's heart was racing as he excitedly made his way there.

He was only in the parking lot about a minute when Carlos came driving up in his black Mercedes. Jackson didn't have time to consider making any changes to his plan. He painted his face with charcoal and wore a baseball cap and dark sunglasses. He looked down at his hands, and they were shaking with anticipation. Before he got out of his car, he nervously said, "Ok, here goes nothing."

As soon as Carlos parked his car, Jackson ran over to it with his pistol and silencer attached in his hand. Just as Carlos opened the door, Jackson put the gun to the back of his head and pulled the trigger. The Rottweiler immediately lunged toward Jackson in attack mode. Carlos' left arm and hand instantly fell to his side and blocked the car door so that it wouldn't close. Jackson tried to push the door shut, but the hand and arm were in the way. He had to deal with the dog trying desperately to get to him.

Unable to shut the door and figure out what to do with the attacking dog simultaneously created a problem. The only thing Jackson could do was leave the door and run for his car. He hoped the dog didn't get to him before he got there. He would have had to kill it and didn't want to shoot the dog.

When Jackson let go of the door, he immediately started running, and the dog was fighting to get past Carlos's body and out of the car. Thankfully, the dog stalled temporarily, just long enough, but began barreling after him, growling and barking. He was able to get in his car just in time as the dog slammed into the driver's side of the vehicle as closed the door. It continued to growl and show its teeth while barking loudly. It was biting at the side mirror and tires as Jackson began to drive away. It followed for about a block until it finally gave up the chase. Jackson watched it in his rearview mirror as it returned to be with Carlos. He said, "Thank goodness, that was too close for comfort."

When he got home, he met with Ashley and told her everything went as she had planned, except that Carlos's dog created a bit of a problem for him.

He nervously laughed and said, "It was a little scary. I didn't have a problem killing Carlos. But if that dog had gotten to me, he would've taken a chunk out of me before I could've killed him."

Ashley replied, "Well, thank goodness we no longer have to worry about Carlos or his men coming after us anymore. Maybe now it's over."

Jackson breathed a massive sigh of relief and said, "Yes, for sure. Thank you for all your help. You have been amazing through all of this. I love you, mom."

***

Chapter 21 - Ashley's Gone

After relaxing for a few days, Jackson decided to call Kari and find out how she had been doing. They agreed to meet downtown and have lunch together. He felt a massive weight lifted off his chest as they laughed and enjoyed each other's company. During lunch, they agreed to go to a movie sometime within the next few weeks.

Ashley went back to her routine at the bar and was once again feeling comfortable about everything. She felt good that she could do her part in getting rid of Carlos and his men. She was relieved that the threat of Carlos trying to kill Jackson was no longer on her mind. She stayed at Sam's place after work on Friday and Saturday nights for the next few weeks and partied with everyone. The illegal drugs she took seemed more relaxing, and she enjoyed the highs even more.

It was an early Saturday morning two weeks after Jackson killed Carlos when he got a knock on his front door. He quickly put on his clothes, peeked outside, and saw two police officers standing nervously on his front porch.

He slowly opened the door and said, "Hello, officers. Can I help you?"

One of the officers said, "Are you Jackson Bailey?"

He said yes, thinking, "Oh, crap, they found out I killed Carlos or maybe some of his men, and they've come to get me."

The officer then said, "Is your mom Ashley?"

Jackson looked him in the eyes and immediately knew something was wrong as he slowly said, "Yes, that's my mom."

The officer then told him his mother's body was in her car in the rough section of town. She was in her car and had died from what appeared to be an apparent drug overdose. He said there were no visible signs of trauma to her body.

Jackson was in denial and shock when he said, "No, you can't be talking about my mom. She is staying at her boyfriend, Sam Freeman's house for the weekend."

The officer opened a wallet, showed him her picture, and said, "Does this look like your mom, and is this her wallet?"

Jackson immediately started to cry, "No, not my mom. Please tell me this isn't true. It can't be her. She's all I have."

The officer told him he could go to the coroner's office and identify her when he was up to doing that. One of the officers asked him if he was going to be ok. Jackson shook his head up and down that he would. Then the officers told him they were sorry for his loss before they left.

Once Jackson closed the door, he fell to his knees and began to sob in deep heartfelt pain. He had his face cupped in his hands. All the years with his mom were rewinding in his head as the tears rolled down his face. He yelled out, "Mom, I love you."

He went to his bedroom, lay on his bed, and cried for a few hours. Then his sadness turned into deep anger as his mom's death began to creep upon him. He wondered what her car was doing parked in that part of town. She never went to that area to get her drugs. She always got them from Sam or some people attending Sam's parties. He also wondered why Sam wasn't with her or why he hadn't called and told him about his mom dying. He asked himself why he had to hear the news from the police, not Sam. He wondered if Sam was also dead.

He took a shower, slowly made his way to his car, and headed to the coroner's office. When he got there and identified her body, he thought she looked different. Her body had a light gray to faint blue color, but it was her.

He never knew he could feel such terrible pain and loss. His heart was broken. She was all he had ever had since he was born. He had never experienced anything like that when he killed all the previous people. The emotion was different; he always thought they deserved what they got, which wasn't personal. Now he was devastated at losing her.

He stayed with her body, held her hands, and told her he loved her repeatedly. After a few hours, the staff had to come and tell him it was time for him to leave.

When he left, he drove straight to Sam's house. He hadn't seen Sam's body at the coroner's office, so he figured he must still be alive. The closer he got to Sam's house, the angrier he became. When he got there, he was in a rage, knocking on the door loudly. After several more times, Sam finally came to the door. He looked as though he was still stoned as he opened the door. He wasn't wearing a shirt; he wore jeans and no shoes. He was smoking a cigarette, and his hair was messy and stringy. For that fleeting moment, Jackson thought he looked just like a strung-out drug addict.

Jackson pushed his way into the house and yelled at Sam, "What the fuck happened to my mom, Sam? How did she die? I want to know. I want answers."

Sam quietly said, "Come over here and sit down and I'll tell you."

Jackson was having a hard time controlling his anger as he said, I don't feel like sitting down, Sam, "You were supposed to watch out for her when she was with you, so what happened? Why was she found in her car in the rough part of town? She never went to that part of town, and you know that's true."

Sam replied, "Your mom and I were sitting on the couch smoking weed and taking a few pills. I passed out, and when I woke up, your mom was lying on the floor, and she wasn't breathing. I tried to revive her, but it was too late. One or two pills she took were laced with Fentanyl or something, killing her. I didn't want her body to be found at my house, or the police would've thrown me in prison for possession of drugs. I waited a little while to sober up a bit. Once I was thinking straight, I put her in her car and had a friend follow me as we drove it to where the police found her. I'm sorry, I didn't know what else to do."

Jackson screamed out, "You call that thinking straight. It's like discarding something you no longer want in your life. She loved you, and you got rid of her like trash."

"Who was your friend with you when you dropped off her car?"

He replied, "It was a friend Delbert Marlow. He was here when it all went down, so he offered to help."

"So why didn't you call me and let me know what happened? Why did you let the police notify me that way?"

Sam replied, "I guess I panicked and was afraid to let the police know I was involved. I thought they would throw me in jail."

Jackson was furious as he said, "I want you to find out who the ones were that gave or sold you those pills that killed her. I'm going to bury my mom, and then when I'm finished, I want the names and addresses of the people involved. If you don't have that information, I will kill you once the funeral is over and then find those people myself. Do you understand me, Sam?"

At first, Sam acted like he was offended by Jackson's tone toward him but realized that Jackson might be serious about killing him. He told Jackson he would get the names and addresses to make him feel better.

Jackson said, "Yes, it will make me feel better."

Sam said, "If it's any consolation, I loved your mom."

Jackson said, "Fuck you, Sam, you let her die. It would've helped if you had taken better care of her. She was all I had in this world, and now she's gone. It should have been you that died and not her."

He blamed Sam for giving his mom the drugs and was so upset that he felt a deep desire to kill Sam. He had to fight his feelings because he knew the police would imprison him for killing Sam. He stood up and stormed toward the door. As he was leaving, he yelled, "I will talk to you at her funeral and get the names I want from you. Don't try to fuck me over, Sam. It would be a terrible mistake for you."

Sam was trying his best to appease Jackson. He thought Jackson was blowing off idle steam, which was his way of dealing with his mom's death. Sam didn't know that Jackson was dead serious about his threat to kill him.

The following week Jackson paid for Ashley's funeral with cash and planned a graveside funeral. They had talked about it, and Ashley told Jackson she wanted to be cremated and not laid in a casket when she died. They didn't have many friends, but Ashley had the people from the bar that knew and liked her that came to the funeral. The entire experience was a solemn and lonely time for him, and he wanted the whole thing to be over. Jackson didn't want to feel the pain anymore. He cried a lot at night as he lay in bed and thought about her. He was thankful they got to spend so much time together when they were going after Carlos and his men. It had bonded them once again.

After the graveside services, Sam returned to Jackson and handed him two men's names that sold him the drugs. Scribbled on the note was each of their addresses. Jackson thanked him for the information and quickly turned and walked away.

**

Chapter 22 - Going after Sam and Delbert

Even though Sam had gotten Jackson the two men's names, he held Sam responsible for his mom's death. He was the one person that was driving Jackson crazy when he thought about her death. He couldn't help how he felt but couldn't forgive Sam for letting his mom take the harmful drugs. He felt Sam should've tested them before giving them to her. Jackson honestly thought he was the one that should have died from taking harmful drugs and not his mom.

While lying in bed one night, Jackson whispered, "I'm sorry, mom, but I have to go after Sam and kill him. I want you to know this one is for me, and I'm not doing it for you. If I don't kill him, I don't think I can live with myself for letting him get away scot-free for your death. I hope you understand and forgive me for what I'm about to do to him."

Over the next few weeks, Jackson carefully planned how to kill Sam and began to put his plan in motion. He waited until a Friday night, and things were back to normal for Sam and his group of friends. Jackson parked his car about a mile away and walked to Sam's house. He had an entire can of gasoline he carried with him. When he arrived around eleven at night, people were back to drinking alcohol and doing their drugs. It was as if nothing had ever happened to Ashley.

When Jackson peeked through the window, he was shocked to see a new girl sitting next to Sam. But more shocking, they were kissing and groping each other. As he stood there and watched, he was furious as he thought, "Yeah, the fool loved my mom, didn't he? It's only been a few weeks since she died, and he already has a new girl. Man, that's some sick stuff."

Then a twisted thought came to his mind, "Maybe he had this girl all along and got rid of my mom on purpose so that he could be with this one." Seeing them making out on the sofa made Jackson even more determined and convinced about killing Sam. He was so angry that he was beside himself and felt he wanted to bust right in and kill him. He would have if he could've gotten away with it.

He waited until everyone had gone home, except for the girl Sam was kissing. They were still doing drugs and making out on the sofa. He was becoming impatient and couldn't stand seeing what Sam and she were doing. As he glared at Sam through the window, he whispered, "What a fucking loser. I don't know what my mom ever saw in you. You're just a worthless piece of shit." He decided to take a walk into the darkness for about twenty minutes. He didn't want to watch them and had to calm his nerves.

It was around three in the morning when the two finally finished with each other and passed out on the couch. Jackson didn't want to kill the girl because he felt she was an innocent part of everything. Because of her, he had to change his plans, and he came up with another plan from his original one.

The doors to Sam's house were always open because people came and went during his party. Jackson had his backpack on with all the gear he carried during an attack. The music was still blaring as he slowly walked into the house. He cautiously shut all the doors to the bedrooms and bathrooms. He made sure nothing got bumped as he approached them on the couch.

The girl was lying with her head at the opposite end of the sofa from Sam. She had her head on the arm of the couch and, curled up in a fetal position, passed out. Jackson hit her with his fits a couple of quick hard blows to make sure she was out. She went limp, and he quickly picked her up and carried her outside the house. After he had her outside, he put duct tape across her eyes and mouth. Then he wrapped it around her feet and hands and tied her hands behind her back. He now had her in a hog-tied position with her feet and knees bent toward her back and hands so she couldn't move. He carried her to her car and carefully placed her on her stomach in the back seat.

Once she couldn't move, he went back into the house, lit two long candles, and placed them near Sam's sofa. He went outside and got the can of gas he'd brought. He went inside and poured the gas all around the sofa's base. He went to the kitchen and turned on all the gas burners on high but didn't light them. He also turned on the gas in the oven and didn't light it either. The gas was spewing out at full force as he waited a few minutes to make sure everything was ready to go.

He took the gas can, left the house, and checked on the girl before leaving. She was breathing, so he knew she would be ok. He cleaned all the fingerprints from the duct tape and the car. He pushed her vehicle away from the house so it wouldn't catch on fire once the house exploded.

He walked briskly back to his car, ensuring nobody had seen him. He got in his car and waited for about two hours before becoming impatient and heading toward Sam's house. Before he got close to it, there was a massive explosion, and the place went up in a huge fireball. Jackson smiled as he quickly drove past the house and went home. Once home, he took the gas can out of his car and put it back in the garage. He also put his backpack in his secret hiding place.

The next day, he heard on the news that a body was in the rubble of a burned house. The report said that it was the home of Sam Freeman. A female survivor was tied up in her car but said she didn't know what happened and never saw the perpetrator who did that.

Jackson didn't want loose ends, so a few days later, he found Delbert Marlow. He worked with Sam in construction and was the one Sam enlisted to help him get rid of Ashley's body. It was Monday and a workday. Jackson had previously found out who he was and what he looked like, so he followed him home from work.

The following day Jackson went to Delbert's home and made sure nobody watched him as he broke into Delbert's house while he was at work. Jackson had been waiting for him when he got home that day from work.

Delbert wasn't expecting anything as he came from the garage into the house. As soon as he opened the door, Jackson put the pistol, with a silencer attached to his head, and pulled the trigger. Jackson whispered, "I'm sorry, but you should have minded your business."

He didn't want to be seen by anyone during the daylight, so he waited a few hours until it got dark before leaving the scene. Once comfortable, he left Delbert's house, walked back to his car about a half-mile away, and drove home.

***

Chapter 23 - Going after Calvin

Travis Watney and Calvin Newman were the two names on the paper that Sam gave Jackson. Once Jackson left the funeral service, he pulled out the paper. He had tears in his eyes as he whispered, "I got these guys, mom. They aren't going to get away with killing you. I'll take care of them for providing you with that poison."

Jackson began to find out where the two men lived and their everyday habits for the next few days. After some research, he found they lived alone and were known as small fish in a big pond in the drug-dealing world. Travis had blond hair, was thirty-three years old, and was buffed from working out at the gym. He had plenty of time to work out because he didn't have a regular job and was free during the day. His only source of income was selling drugs at night.

He traveled in the nightclub and bar scene and always had his two pretty blond-haired girls with him. They gave Travis sex whenever he wanted in return for the drugs they used. They stayed stoned most of the time they were with him. The girls liked hanging out with him because he provided them with drugs and bought whatever they wanted. It also made them feel important, like they were with a celebrity.

The girls were almost always with him during his drug runs. He felt they helped him with his drug dealing because they were a distraction for the people he was doing business with. The blonds stayed with him many nights except on Mondays and Tuesdays when they spent time at their homes. The only time they stayed with him during those two nights was when they were too stoned to drive home. He was a good-looking guy who always had plenty of drugs and money. For those reasons, he always had young girls who were more than willing to come home with him.

Calvin was Travis's co-distributor but worked for Travis. Calvin was the one that did all the dirty work that needed to be done, like collecting money when someone wouldn't pay. He was also a thin white guy and around thirty-eight years old with long dark brown hair. He was already starting to show gray around the sides of his head. He was also a drug addict, so all the money he made from Travis went toward his drug habit.

Calvin would come over on Mondays, help Travis count the money, and take care of other business for Travis. Sometimes Travis would have to get on Calvin for doing too many drugs on the weekends. He would sometimes be too hungover to do his job on Mondays. Jackson believed Monday after killing Calvin would be the best time for him to go after Travis. He didn't want to try and kill both of them simultaneously because he felt like it was too risky. He thought it would be better to catch Calvin while still stoned and at home on a Sunday.

Calvin lived in an older mobile home park in the northern part of town. He lived in a smaller single-wide trailer with a living room, small kitchen, bathroom, and bedroom. He was a sloppy housekeeper, so things and dishes piled up in the sink were out of place.

Jackson slowly drove into the mobile home park and looked things over before coming up with a plan. People walked around, and neighbors visited each other throughout the park. Several savory-looking people occasionally went to Calvin's house to pick up their drugs.

When he drove back into the park after dark, the activity had died down, and the people were inside their homes. After watching Calvin's house for a while, Jackson decided he would go after him around ten in the evening on a Sunday. After killing Calvin, he would go to Travis's home early the following day.

Jackson began putting his plan into place as he went on the street looking for a stray dog. He spent an entire day trying to locate one he felt would work for what he had planned. Once Jackson had the dog he thought was perfect, he brought it home, fed it, and watered him. He then set up a bed for him in the garage for the night. Not wanting to get too attached to the dog, he kept it outside the house.

The next day he went to the store and purchased a leash for the dog. He went to his friends in the streets and bought a bottle of illegal fentanyl pills. The pills were expensive, but Jackson didn't care what they cost. The guy told Jackson, "You better be careful with those things. It doesn't take too many to kill you. Maybe only a couple of them." Jackson winched and said, "Yeah, I know." Once he had everything he needed, he was ready to go after the two men.

The following Sunday night, he put his backpack in his car along with his loaded pistols. He grabbed the fentanyl pills, put the dog in the car, and headed toward Calvin's house. He parked his car in the back of a McDonald's parking lot, then got out and looked around. He had his sweatshirt with his hoody pulled over his head. It was nine-thirty at night, and the parking lot was empty and quiet. He stuck the pistol, with the silencer attached, in his belt and under his sweatshirt. He put the leash on the dog and then locked his car. He made sure he had the fentanyl pills in his pants pocket and then headed to the mobile home park a half-mile away.

When he got there, it was quiet, and there was no activity in the park. The entire place seemed to be shut down for the night as he made his way to the house. He appeared to be just a guy taking his dog for a walk. He let the dog stop a few times to sniff around and raise its leg to pee.

When he came to Calvin's home, the light was on in the living room. Jackson looked around to make sure nobody was watching him as he peeked through the window. He saw Calvin sitting in a beat-up recliner, looking like he was sleeping. Jackson was a little nervous as he approached Calvin's front door. He knocked a few times to wake Calvin, and he stumbled to the door after a few minutes.

He opened the door, and before Jackson could say anything, he said, "It's after hours. You'll have to come back later." He started to shut the door and sit back down.

Jackson quickly replied, "No, I'm not here for that, I have this dog I found, and I was wondering if it was yours."

When he said that, he let go of the leash and let the dog quickly run inside. When the dog did that, Jackson stepped inside the trailer as if to retrieve the dog.

Calvin said, "No, that isn't my fucking dog, so get him the fuck out of here."

Jackson pulled out his gun, pointed it at Calvin, and said, "I know it's not your dog, dumbass. I want you to sit down in your recliner, or I'll kill you where you're standing. Do you understand me?"

Calvin seemed shocked as he stood there for a minute, trying to process what Jackson was saying. Jackson had to tell him again to sit down, or he would kill him.

Calvin then realized what was happening and quickly sat down in the recliner. Jackson shut the door and sat on the sofa next to him. The entire time he had his gun pointed at Calvin.

He said, "You know, Calvin, I'm going to kill you tonight, but I'm not going to let you suffer. I'll let you die the way you would love to go. From taking drugs."

Calvin said, "Why? Who are you, and what did I do to you?"

Jackson replied, "My name doesn't matter. It wouldn't mean anything to you anyway. It wasn't me you hurt with your drugs. You and Travis sold some to a guy I know, and he gave them to my mom, and the pills killed her. Now you're going to die the same way as she did."

Calvin said, "Hey, I never meant to kill anybody. I was selling drugs and doing my job."

Jackson quietly said, "It's ok, Calvin. It will be painless for you."

Calvin started to yell out, and Jackson hit him in the head with the butt of the pistol. He knocked him temporarily unconscious. When he came to Jackson was angry as he said, "You do that again, and I'll shoot you in the head and be finished with you. You stupid fuck."

Calvin had a half-filled glass of soda on an end table next to his chair. Jackson pulled out the fentanyl pills and handed Calvin several of them.

He said, "Now I want you to take these and don't try to spit them out, or you'll be dead."

Calvin's eyes got large, and he asked, "What are those things?"

Jackson chuckled and said, "Just something to help you sleep, but more like a permanent sleep."

Calvin began to resist and told Jackson he wouldn't take them. He started to stand up like he wanted to fight Jackson, so he hit Calvin in the head again with the butt of the pistol.

Calvin started to scream, so Jackson pushed him back in his chair, put the gun to his head, and said, "You do that again, and you're a dead man. Keep your mouth shut and take the fucking pills. I'm not going to tell you again."

Calvin then started taking the pills one by one. Jackson wasn't sure how many it would take to kill him, but he made him take several of them.

After a while, Calvin stiffened in his chair, his eyes rolled back in his head, and he stopped breathing. White foam was coming out of his mouth. Jackson went over to him and felt for a pulse; Calvin didn't have one. He was dead.

He grabbed the leash of the dog, and they left. On the way back to his car, Jackson turned the dog loose. He rubbed his head and ears and said, "You did good, boy. You're a good dog. Thank you for your help tonight."

***

Chapter 24 - Going after Travis

Travis got all of his drugs from a huge dealer by the name of Manny Fernandez. He had a warehouse in the rough part of town where he sold to dealers like Travis. The police left Manny alone unless they got pressure from higher up to do something about the operation. Manny had several thugs that worked for him, and they would kill anyone that Manny asked them to kill. The police didn't want to confront the group because they knew it would end up in a gun battle, and officers could be injured or killed. If they forced it to close down, Manny would temporarily open it in another location and continue distributing the drugs from there.

Jackson felt Manny Fernandez and his operation were ultimately responsible for his mom's death. He knew he would go after Manny's operation when he got the chance. But, for now, Jackson just wanted the ones he felt were directly involved in his mom's death. After he killed Sam, Delbert, and Calvin, he tried to kill Travis. He and Calvin were the ones that sold the drugs to Sam.

Travis had his own house in a nice middle-class neighborhood. It was a three-bedroom, two-bathroom house, and most of his nearby neighbors knew he was a drug dealer. They left him alone because he always kept to himself and never bothered them or peddled his drugs from home.

Jackson began to follow Travis to find out his routine. He wanted to know where he was and what he had done all day. He found the two blonds stayed at their places during the first few days of the week. Travis did most of his deliveries and banking from the middle to the end of the week. Things were pretty uneventful at the beginning of the week, but it got pretty crazy with people partying and doing drugs at his house by the weekend. Jackson thought this must have been the way these guys and Sam had met. They lived very similar lifestyles with partying and drugs.

Calvin would come over on Mondays and give Travis the money he collected from the clients. He also helped Travis count the money and take care of other businesses for Travis. Sometimes Travis would have to get on Calvin for doing too many drugs on the weekends. He would be a little too hungover to do his job on Mondays. Jackson had already determined that Mondays would be the best time for him to go after Travis.

The following day after he killed Calvin, Jackson made it to Travis's house. It was still dark as he parked several blocks away and grabbed his gear. Once at Travis's home, he quietly broke into the house.

After he was inside, he began to slowly go through the house, just like he had done on a lot of his house thefts. He crept to each bedroom, slowly opened the door, and looked around. He didn't go to the master bedroom where Travis was sleeping because he wanted to make sure nobody else was in the house before he confronted him.

When he was convinced there was nobody else in the house, he directed his attention toward the master bedroom. He slowly made his way to the bed where Travis was lying with the cover pulled up to his neck.

He tip-toed over to Travis, put his pistol to his head, and said, "Wake up, Travis. Wake up, buddy."

Travis immediately jumped up in bed and said, "What the fuck."

Jackson softly said, "It's your lucky day, mother fucker. It's the day you're going to die."

Travis was still half asleep and wasn't sure if someone was pulling on him this kind of prank. He said, "Hey Calvin, what the hell are you doing? This is no time to be joking around. I'm still sleeping."

Jackson calmly said, "Oh, I'm sorry, Travis, this is no joke, and your friend Calvin. He's dead. I killed him."

Then Travis realized this was no joke and it was real. Thinking Jackson was robbing him, he said, "Who are you, and what do you want? If you want money, it's over there in the drawer. You can take all but leave me alone."

Jackson said, "You dumb, mother fucker Travis. Do you think I would go through all this trouble just for money?"

He motioned for Travis to get out of bed and said, "Get your ass out of bed and head toward your kitchen. Don't try anything stupid, or I'll kill you right where you stand."

Travis slowly got out of bed and asked, "Is it ok if I put on my pants?"

Jackson replied, "No, there won't be any need for them. Just keep walking."

When they got to the kitchen, Jackson had him sit in a dining chair with a back. He had him put his hands behind his back and the chair. Jackson quickly grabbed the duct tape from his backpack and wrapped it around Travis's hands and the chair. Just as he started to put some around his feet, Travis began kicking and fighting to stand. Jackson quickly hit him in the head with the butt of the pistol and knocked him unconscious. While he was out, Jackson wrapped Travis's feet with tape and then around the chair. Once secure, he grabbed another chair and sat down across from Travis. He whispered, "What's with these guys, they have a gun pointed at their head, and they want to try and fight me. It's just bizarre."

When he woke up, Jackson had the gun pointed at him and smiled as he said, "Now, wasn't that fun? You want to try it again, dumbass?"

Travis said, "If you don't want my money, what do you want? I haven't done anything to you. I don't even know you."

Jackson slowly said, "I know you don't know me, but I know you. I want to kill you, just like you killed my mom."

Travis replied, "I don't know what you're talking about. I've never killed anyone in my life."

Jackson said, "I beg to differ with you, Travis. Do you think that nobody has ever died from all the drugs you've sold to people throughout your lifetime?" He didn't give Travis time to answer as he said, "The drugs you sold to my mom's boyfriend Sam ended up killing her. So yes, you have killed someone. You killed my mom."

When Jackson said that, his eyes widened because he recognized Sam. He said, "I only sold him a few pills occasionally."

Jackson said, "What fucking difference do you think that makes, one or a thousand? It's all the same to me. She's still dead, mother fucker."

When Travis finally realized Jackson wanted to kill him and couldn't talk his way out of it, he started apologizing and pleading for his life.

Jackson took out the bottle of Fentanyl and said, "This is how you're going to die. Just like my mom, but don't worry, it will be painless for you, just like it was for Calvin. I won't blow your brains out of your head and all over your beautiful kitchen."

Travis changed his demeanor and started yelling and telling Jackson that he was crazy and that if he got loose, he would kill him. Jackson went over, put the gun behind his ear, and whispered, "Do you think I'm going to turn you loose? Do you want me to shoot you in the head, or do you want to take a chance on your non-killer pills? If you don't stop yelling, you won't have to worry about it. I'll just put a bullet in your head and be done with you." Travis then relaxed as if he had resigned himself to die one way or the other.

Jackson went to the kitchen cabinet, grabbed a glass, and filled it halfway with water. He then went back to Travis and told him to lean his head back and open his mouth. He reluctantly did as told. Jackson poured four pills into his mouth, gave him a drink of water, and made him swallow them. He repeated it again, sat down in the chair, and waited for the drugs to take effect.

Within a few minutes, Travis began to throw up. Jackson quickly grabbed a towel and caught the throw-up before it hit the floor. He waited a few minutes and then repeated everything once again. Then he sat back down in the chair across from him again and waited for the drugs to take effect.

It didn't take long, and Travis's body began to jerk violently, and after a few minutes, he went limp. Jackson felt for a pulse, but there was none. He wiped his fingerprints from the glass, took off the duct tape from Travis, and wiped it clean. He took the towel, washed it out, and then went to the laundry room and put it in the washer.

He unwrapped Travis from the chair and pulled his body back to the master bedroom. He rolled up all the duct tape and put it back into his bag. He then carried him and put him back in bed. He threw the cover over him and wiped his fingerprints off the bottle of fentanyl. It still had a couple in it as he laid it next to Travis's body. Once he finished, he went back to his car while still dark and quickly left.

***

Chapter 25 - Five Years Later

Standing in front of the mirror, Jackson was beaming with pride. He thought the new DEA uniform looked incredible on him. He whispered, "Hey, mom, I did it. I did what you always wanted: I got a college degree and a real job." He was twenty-three years old, standing six feet tall, and one hundred and ninety pounds of pure muscle. He had just landed a job with the Federal Government's Drug Enforcement Agency branch.

After killing Travis, he decided he would take some of the cash he had stashed away and enroll in the Criminal Justice program at Bakersfield College. He got the house free and clear from his mom and didn't have any payments, taxes, or insurance. It was the perfect time for him to go to school, so he went to Bakersfield College for four years and received his BS degree in Criminology. His GPA during college was 3.8 on average for the entire four years. While going to school, he used two thousand per month of Carlos' money to care for his financial needs. He didn't have to work unless he wanted.

He took his education to the next level and became a DEA agent. To become an agent, he had to be twenty-one years of age, have a BS degree, and have a GPA of 2.95. He had those qualifications, so he finished the DEA training for 18 weeks in Quantico, Virginia.

In the back of Jackson's mind, becoming a DEA would give him the perfect cover to go after the person he held ultimately responsible for his mom's death. It was Manny Fernandez and his group of thugs. He was amazed they were still the largest distributors of drugs in Bakersfield, even after all the time he was going through college and DEA training. He would take his time before doing anything with Manny and his men. It might take him a year or even two, but he had already waited over five years, so he would be patient and do it the right way.

After his mom's death, Jackson stopped smoking pot and doing drugs. He had been clean and sober for over five years. He now hated anything and anyone involved in the drug trafficking business. His hatred for it became the driving force behind all his hard work for the past five years. Thankfully, he was smart enough to mask his contempt for drug dealers during all the psychological tests he took during his DEA training. He lied and said he never did drugs because it was a prerequisite for the DEA agent job. He also began to date Kari regularly and didn't want her to know he did any drugs.

He had requested to remain in Bakersfield once he landed the DEA job because he and Kari had dated all through college and training. During that period, she got her degree in nursing at Bakersfield College while he got his in Criminology.

She could go to work at San Joaquin Community Hospital after she got out of school. She was always busy as a full-time nurse, and his job demanded a lot of his time. The two of them committed that they would marry someday when it worked out for them. Jackson never told her about his past and the people he killed. He kept everything that happened to him in the past to himself.

He never told her that he felt he could kill someone legally and not go to jail for killing them. He just had to make sure killing them looked as though it was during a time they were involved in some criminal activity. The school had taught him restraint, but he wasn't sure he could follow that guideline when they sent him after a targeted person.

Not long after he graduated from the DEA training, he received orders to report to Los Angeles to join up with several other DEA agents. The DEA had made arrangements for all the agents to stay at a specific hotel. Before leaving, he told Kari he wasn't sure how long he would be gone but would keep in touch with her and let her know.

The DEA leader told them they would take down a massive drug trafficking ring when he got there. They had been following two Mexican men that had slipped across the border into the United States. They were Ricardo Estaban Vasquez and Benito Juaquez Marquez, both in their late twenties to early thirties. The two men were members of one of the largest Mexican drug Cartels in Mexico

The Cartel had a massive shipment of methamphetamines, heroin, cocaine, and fentanyl heading to Los Angeles, New York, Chicago, Houston, and Atlanta.

That particular Cartel controls about two-thirds of the drug trade in the US. They prey on addicts and on small towns where they infiltrate the towns. They promise to hope to the people but deliver the opposite, despair. Their drugs have fueled the opioid crisis, homelessness, and overdoses in the US for years and are big business. They are a very violent group that has attacked law enforcement in Mexico. They carry machine guns and hand grenades and try to eliminate their rivals so they don't have any competition.

The DEA knew who the two men were because they had been under surveillance for six months. The DEA had let them come freely across the border because they wanted to know the drug's ultimate destination. With wiretaps and undercover operatives, the DEA followed them to a home in an upper-class neighborhood.

The men stayed in a sizeable Colonial-style home with beautiful palm trees and manicured yard. The home's main person was merely a manager of the stash house for the cartel. He wasn't a distributor for them but got paid well for his services.

Once the DEA had the information they needed, they assembled their agents at a makeshift command center at the hotel. After receiving their instructions, the team loaded up in two vehicles and headed to the house's location. They parked several blocks away, got out, suited up, and put on their helmets and tactical gear. They carried battering rams, bolt cutters, and heavy weaponry with them.

Jackson was a rookie in the group and was excited to be part of the team. They wanted to break him into their operation method, so they had him join them. He was happy they had each other to back up the DEA actions. He hoped they could kill a few of the cartel members and stop some drug trafficking in the US.

It was still dark outside when they reached their intended destination, with the only light being the streetlights. Once at the house, they fanned out and took cover around the home's entire exterior.

The group leader told Jackson and an undercover operative to follow him. He then banged loudly on the front door.

He said in a loud voice, "DEA Search Warrant!" Not getting an answer, he banged loudly on door two more times and said, "DEA, agents, Search Warrant!" At that moment, the task force agents broke down the front door.

A man was standing inside the vast foyer with a confused and angry look. The DEA leader handed him the search warrant as he,

Jackson, and the other agent quickly went inside with their weapons drawn.

Ricardo Vasquez came running into the room and had an automatic weapon in his hands. He started to raise the gun and fire it at the DEA team when the other agent quickly shot and killed him. Benito Marquez also came running into the room and fired his automatic weapon in the team's direction within a few minutes. The team leader got hit in the left arm with one of his bullets. Jackson and the other agent quickly returned to the fire and killed Marquez. Jackson immediately went to the man standing in the foyer and threw him to the ground. He put the man's hands behind his back and quickly cuffed him.

They yelled to see if the team leader was ok, and he said he was and for them to check the rest of the house. As the rest of the team moved in, they went slowly throughout the house and found several others hiding, but they gave up without fighting. Once everything was under control, they returned to check on the team leader. He quickly rushed out to receive medical aid for his wound.

Jackson was a little disappointed that the entire ordeal was over too soon. However, they had accomplished their goal and shut the operation down. They had the house manager in custody, and they could take him back to headquarters and interrogate him. They believed they would find out where all the drugs were and where other cartel places and men were in the United States. They had also collected several million dollars of cash, over a thousand kilos of meth, and about a hundred pounds of cocaine, heroin, fentanyl, and other drugs.

Jackson gained confidence and respect from the other DEA agents for his professional attitude and shooting ability. He was happy the other agents felt that way about him, but his job was getting drug traffickers off the streets. Jackson figured they would be back on the roads within a few days if all they did was arrest them. He was more interested in killing them to get them off the streets than arresting them.

Chapter 26 – Going after Manny Fernandez

Once the operation was over, Jackson returned to Bakersfield to await further orders from the DEA for his next duty. He spent some time with Kari and told her all about what happened during the drug bust. They also spent much time together, going to dinner and lunch when convenient with her schedule.

While home, he secretly began to plan how he could go after Manny's group and do it legally and under the protection of a DEA agent. He wasn't going to let Kari know the motivation behind his operation. He also wasn't going to tell her it had nothing to do with the DEA. It was about his revenge for his mom's death. She was always working long hours and then coming home and sleeping most of the time at home. It was perfect for Jackson because it gave him the freedom he needed.

He began to do surveillance on the Wearhouse where Manny had his operation. The Wearhouse was an old 20,000-square-foot concrete building built in the 1940s in the industrial area of town. The interior was open, beamed V-shaped wooden roof covered with shingles. Many homeless people made their homes in a few abandoned buildings nearby.

He found a hiding place in some thick bushes across the road from the Wearhouse, where he had a good view of the building. He was in a spot that would be hard to see or find unless you were looking for something in the bushes. He had binoculars and watched every one that came into and out of place all day. He also watched them at night to see if the activity continued. He found that almost all the action was during the day—the men who counted and distributed the drugs and money left around six daily. When Kari asked why he was spending time away at night, he told her it was just DEA work.

From what Jackson could tell, Manny's operation was large, with around ten Cartel types of men carrying automatic weapons. They monitored everyone in and out of the Wearhouse as they searched them for weapons. Jackson was familiar with these people and knew they were ready to use their guns if someone did something out of line with them. He had faced this with Carlos and his men several years earlier.

Jackson spent about two weeks just watching the place every day. He was careful not to run into any of the homeless people that lived in the area. He discovered what Manny looked like as he watched him with his binoculars when he arrived and left each day. He always had a couple of heavily armed bodyguards with him as they drove up and left in a late-model black Mercedes. He went to the Wearhouse every day around the same time of day. When Jackson first saw him, his contempt for him was almost overwhelming. He wanted nothing more than to put a bullet in Manny's head.

He talked to his immediate supervisor at the DEA and asked if they would be interested in raiding a large drug trafficking operation in Bakersfield. The agent told him it was too small for them to go through the process of shutting it down. He said they were more interested in the more prominent distributors where they felt they could hurt the Cartels the most. He told him that the local police and other law enforcement agencies could handle operations of that size.

Jackson knew the local police wouldn't do anything about the operation. They had turned their backs on it for as long as he could remember. After working with the DEA, Jackson realized the local police didn't know how to go after an operation like Manny's without many police offers getting killed. He knew it wouldn't be easy to do it alone but believed he had to try, even if he got killed in the process.

He went on a few more raids with the DEA over several months and gained much experience. He collected several automatic weapons during the attacks and took them and some ammunition home with him. Some of the other agents teased him about starting a war with someone. One of his fellow agents said, "What the hell are you going to do with all the weapons and ammo, Jackson?" Are you planning to go to war with someone?"

He said, "No, I just like collecting them. Who knows, maybe the government will try to take away our guns someday, or we may have a revolution here in the United States. If either of those things happens, I want to be ready."

When he went after Manny's group, he didn't tell anyone he had plans for all the weapons. He kept the guns hidden away so Kari wouldn't find them.

When he was home, he seemed obsessed with Manny and his operation but never let Kari know how he felt. He knew he was no match for all the guns Manny had to protect his business, so he had to find another way to even the playing field.

At one point, he decided to follow the Mercedes and find out where Manny lived. As the Mercedes got close to a vast 10,000-square-foot mansion, the gates automatically opened, and it drove into the well-groomed circle drive. A large fountain with water ran in the middle of the circle drive. The house was a Spanish-style home with different leveled flat roofs, painted a light terracotta color. Large palm trees, beautiful lush bushes, and flowering plants lined the circle drive and the walled-in property.

He noticed two large Doberman dogs running toward the gates as they opened. They were barking friendly as the Mercedes entered. Jackson whispered, "Wow! So, this is how the rich and famous live? Well, maybe not so famous, but you might be after I kill you."

He believed cameras would be placed throughout the house and property because it was heavily fortified and attacked dogs. The site was more like a fortress than a home. He had to do some soul-searching on what he was going to do to get to Manny. He wasn't sure if he wanted to try and kill him at the Wearhouse with all his guards or figure out how to get inside his large home. All he knew was that he wouldn't wait long and would soon be going after him.

He spent the next several days coming up with a plan of attack. After careful thought, he decided to hit the Wearhouse, where all the drugs and men were located, instead of Manny's home. He believed that the local law enforcement would come in after he killed him and find all the drugs and money in the Wearhouse.

Once he made up his mind about what he would do, he got all his gear ready. The night before his planned attack, he left his house in the middle of the night. He headed for the Wearhouse. He carried a bag full of grenades he'd gotten in Los Angeles. He took as many as he could comfortably carry and four of the automatic weapons he'd confiscated. He had the automatic weapons loaded with full ammunition magazines in each one.

When he arrived at the Wearhouse, he parked his car about a half-mile away and walked the rest of the way to his regular hiding place. He sat his gear down and observed the building for a few hours to see if any activity was happening inside. The building appeared locked up for the night, so he grabbed his gear and slowly made his way toward the building. He moved in a crouched position as he got closer to the Wearhouse.

Once there, he took his time and walked around the back of the building. He kept looking around to make sure there wasn't anyone watching or following him. The place was extremely dark, quiet, and creepy from the back of the building. He went up to one of the windows and peeked inside. He didn't see anyone, so he broke a small hole in the window, just big enough to get his hand in and release the lock. Unlocking it, he slid it open and left it that way for several minutes. He was making sure someone wasn't hiding in the building and heard him break the window. He ducked below the window and waited to see if someone approached. When he realized there wasn't anyone coming after him, he slowly and carefully sat his gear inside the window and then made his way through the window.

Once inside, he took his time and walked through the building. He was careful that nothing fell to the floor as he passed. After a few minutes, he found Manny's office. He took out one of the grenades and left it hidden to retrieve it the following night during his attack. He took his time and found places to hide the four machine guns in strategic locations about twenty feet apart. He wanted them to be easy to retrieve but hidden from the guards if he needed them. He left two grenades next to each of the guns to use them if he had to. He stayed inside the building for about an hour and looked everything over to feel for the installation. Once he felt comfortable, he left through the same window and closed it behind him.

He went home and got some much-needed sleep. It was the middle of the afternoon when he awoke, so he lay around the rest of the evening. He was trying to relax as he went over everything in his head. He knew he would need as much rest as possible because he would be up most of the night.

When Kari came home from work, she asked him what he was doing. He told her he was relaxing because he had to go out on a drug bust later that night. He took a few quick knaps until it was time for him to get ready to leave.

At midnight, he grabbed all his gear and put some more grenades in his bag. He put on his Kevlar vest and his DEA uniform before heading out. When he got there, he parked his vehicle in the same place as the previous days and nights and carefully made his way to the Wearhouse. He went through the same window he'd gone through the night before and closed it behind him.

Once inside, he slowly crept from place to place until he made it to Manny's office once again. He retrieved the grenade he'd hidden the night before and carefully removed the pin. He held onto the handle so it wouldn't explode. He went over to Manny's desk and slowly placed the grenade in the middle drawer with the handle firmly held so it wouldn't explode until the drawer opened. He put the grenade on a small rag with part of it hanging out of the drawer. He was hoping Manny would grab the rag and pull on it, and when he did that, it would force his drawer open. The grenade would then go off right in Manny's face. He looked down at his hands and noticed them trembling slightly after putting the grenade in place. He took a few deep breaths and let them out slowly to calm his nerves. He whispered, "Man, that was a little scary."

He stopped at the bathroom briefly to relieve himself before continuing. He found a hiding place the workers didn't use, and it was between where he'd hidden the four automatic weapons and grenades. He would have to stay hidden in that position for four or five hours until Manny arrived.

He could see everything in the building from his chosen hiding place. The window he'd come through was behind him if he had to use it as an emergency escape. He had several grenades out of his bag and placed them on a metal file cabinet next to where he would hide. They were ready to pull the pins and throw them toward his intended targets when he was ready.

He walked around the building inside the building to familiarize himself with escape routes and other details. He stopped and checked some of the counting and distribution tables for a minute and noticed some illegal drugs stored in and under them. He grimaced in anger and gritted his teeth when he first saw them.

Just before daylight and the arrival of the first workers, he went to the hiding place and got ready. Sitting there waiting, he thought about his mom and how much she meant to him. He had a few tears in his eyes and was wiping them away. He whispered, "I love you, mom. If these guys kill me, I will be with you soon."

The sun had just started to show itself, and there was a chill in the air as the first workers made their way into the building. They laughed and talked loudly to each other, and their voices sounded like echoes to Jackson in the vast room. He nervously kept an eye on them as the workers showed up one by one. Four guards also started showing up around the same time. They had the familiar automatic weapons strapped over their shoulders as they briefly searched the building. Jackson had to be patient and not kill them. He will only open fire on them if they get too close and discover he is there. His main target, and reason for the attack, was Manny.

It was around mid-morning, and Jackson was getting a little antsy when Manny's Mercedes pulled into his familiar parking spot. As he made his way into the building, he had four armed guards. Jackson thought, "Look at this guy. He thinks he's important because he was strutting around and giving orders to everyone." He went to where the workers were busy and shouted a few orders before heading into his office.

Jackson waited with great anticipation for the sound he was hoping to hear. He didn't have to wait long and listened to the grenade explosion in Manny's office. The sound seemed to resonate with the entire building. A couple of the guards ran into the office with their weapons drawn and yelled out when they saw Manny's body. He was almost blown into two pieces because the grenade went above his waist. His head and upper body took the full impact of the grenade. Blood and flesh were all over the floor and wall behind the desk.

As soon as the men came running out of the office, Jackson began to pull the pins to the grenades. He threw two of them in their direction. He then turned and threw two more at the other two guards heading for Manny's office. The people counting the money and the drugs quickly grabbed their weapons and began firing in the direction where Jackson had thrown the grenades. He promptly removed the pins on two more grenades and threw them toward the workers.

The building was covered in smoke from the grenades and gunfire in just a few minutes. Four or five people were not killed in Jackson's initial onslaught of grenades. They kept firing their automatic weapons in the area where they believed Jackson was hiding. He stayed low as he began to move from that position to another, where he had a hidden weapon and grenades. He was firing his gun in the direction of the people still firing at him. He threw the two grenades toward the workers firing them at him. The entire time of the battle, the wounded were screaming and yelling out in pain. Some were cursing and saying they were going to kill him.

He took careful aim and killed two more of them. At that time, he felt the sting of a bullet that caught him in the left shoulder. It stunned him temporarily because he'd never been shot before and didn't realize how it felt. Once he saw the blood, he knew a bullet had hit him. He snapped out of it and continued to fight back.

He crawled to the next spot, where he had a weapon and two grenades hidden. He put one of the grenades between his legs, pulled the pin with his uninjured arm, and threw it in the worker's position. He did the same thing with the second grenade. He emptied the magazine of its bullets and quickly crawled to his next hidden weapon and grenades. He only had two guards left firing at him, but he took a round to the leg during his move. Now he had a bullet wound in his arm and leg but had to keep fighting, or he'd die.

As he got to his next weapon, he did the same thing with the grenades and threw them toward the two men firing at him. After he did that, the firing then stopped. Jackson slowly started trying to get to his feet as he stumbled a few times to get his balance on the injured leg. It was a horrendous battle that lasted over fifteen minutes.

He heard sirens coming in his direction as he slowly turned around to ensure everyone was dead. That's when one of the mortally injured guards raised and took desperation's last shot at him. It hit him on the side of the head and knocked him unconscious. He next remembered waking up a short time while the ambulance took him to the hospital.

The ambulance paramedic said, "You got lucky this time. That bullet just glanced off your skull. If it would've been another quarter-inch deeper, you would be going to the morgue instead of the hospital." Jackson replied, "Yay, lucky me." Then he passed out again. The paramedic continued to bandage his wounded shoulder and leg.

As Jackson lay in the hospital bed the next day, recuperating from his wounds, Kari was by his side as he watched the local news. It said, "Local DEA agent, Jackson Bailey, takes down a major drug dealer, and twelve of his men believed to be part of a huge drug Cartel from Mexico were killed in the attack. Seized in the bust were millions of dollars in cash and several pounds of cocaine, meth, fentanyl, and illegal other drugs."

Since Jackson was wearing his DEA uniform during the attack, the DEA claimed he was working undercover. They said he followed the agency's direction during his raid on the primary drug ring. Jackson knew it wasn't true but wouldn't say anything different. He was ok with the DEA taking credit for the raid because it kept him out of trouble.

After watching the news report, Jackson whispered where Kari couldn't hear him, "Ok, mom, I got the last one. It took me a while, but I got him. It's over now."

He then turned and kissed Kari and said, "Don't you think it's time we get married soon?"

She laughed and replied, "Yeah, like I want to be married to a guy that tries to get himself killed." She hugged him and said, "Yes, of course. I was beginning to wonder if you'd ever ask."

He went from satisfying his acts of revenge by killing the person he felt was ultimately responsible for his mom's death to becoming a local hero.

***

Special Thanks

I want to give a special thanks to Rita Toews for developing the book's cover for me.
Rita Toews of www.yourebookcover.com

***

Other Books by Ron L. Carter

Twenty-One Months – non-fiction

From the Darkness of my Mind – fiction

Unearthly Realms – fiction

The American Terrorist – A Grandfather's Revenge - fiction

The American Terrorist – The Revenge Continues - fiction

Night Crawlers – fiction

Night Crawlers – Reign of Terror – fiction

Accidental Soldiers – fiction

Love me now, don't wait - Poetry

***

Other Books by Ron L. Carter and H.R. Carter

In Defense of Mankind – fiction

Zak Thomas – the Monster Hunter – fiction

Lost Waters - fiction

Made in the USA
Las Vegas, NV
10 January 2024

84094940R00090